SKYJACK!

Rick shot off on his skyboard again, with Tom zooming in pursuit. Tom felt as if he were on the crest of a monster wave of energy, always on the brink of falling. He upped his speed again.

"Hey, guys," Sandra's voice cut in over their earphones. "You're doing ninety!"

"Time to bail out!" Tom yelled, fighting his controls.

"I can't!" Rick's voice was tight. "My foot strap is stuck."

A black shape came whispering out of the sky. Through his infrared visor, Tom recognized an attack helicopter, painted and modified for a stealth mission.

The chopper dropped like a striking hawk. A net flew out to catch Rick and his board in midair.

Rick was gone!

TOM SWIFT 1

THE BLACK DRAGON

VICTOR APPLETON

AN ARCHWAY PAPERBACK
Published by POCKET BOOKS
New York   London   Toronto   Sydney   Tokyo   Singapore

AN ARCHWAY PAPERBACK *Original*

An Archway Paperback published by
POCKET BOOKS, a division of Simon & Schuster
1230 Avenue of the Americas, New York, NY 10020

Copyright © 1991 by Simon & Schuster

Produced by Byron Preiss Visual Publications, Inc.
Special thanks to Bill McCay

ISBN: 0-671-67823-X

First Archway Paperback printing April 1991

10 9 8 7 6 5 4 3 2 1

TOM SWIFT, AN ARCHWAY PAPERBACK and colophon
are registered trademarks of Simon & Schuster.

Cover art by Carla Sormanti

Printed in the U.S.A.

IL 6+

THE BLACK DRAGON

1

"DON'T TELL ME I LOOK LIKE A GEEK," TOM Swift warned his friend Rick Cantwell. But he was grinning as he spoke into the microphone built into his crash helmet.

Tom knew he looked—well, weird. Besides the helmet that covered his blond hair, he was wearing heavy pads at his knees, elbows, and shoulders to protect his lean form. But weirdest of all were the heavy straps that bound his feet to an oversize surfboard, miles from any beach.

"I wouldn't say geek." Rick Cantwell's chuckle came clearly through Tom's earphones. "I'd say ner-r-r-r—"

His voice went into a stutter as Tom twisted a dial on the control panel at his waist. The surfboard under Tom's feet started humming loudly, then floated three feet off the ground.

Rick ran a hand through his sandy brown hair, finally getting his voice back. "This is— I can't even say. It's like magic!"

"Not magic—electricity," Tom said, laughing. "Let's try it out."

He twisted a dial on the control panel. The humming grew louder, and the board sped up, skimming over the putty brown track on the ground. The track—a specially designed electromagnetic carpet—was just as important as the board. When the carpet powered up, it produced a giant electromagnetic field, which "pushed" against the superconductive material in the skyboard, making it float.

"Okay, now," Tom said, turning up the dial. "Let's see how it moves."

The board picked up speed, riding on an invisible wave of magnetism. Tom bent forward a little, like a surfer playing a wave.

"It's like something out of a comic book. Look at that sucker go!" Rick yelled as Tom flashed past. "How fast can you push it?"

Tom shook his head. Typical Rick, he thought.

Rick Cantwell was Tom's best friend. They were classmates at Jefferson High, and as quarterback on the school's football team,

Rick had proven himself strong and brave enough to test any of Tom's inventions.

"The problem with you, Rick, is you've got a reckless streak," Tom told him. "For you, there's only one setting worth trying—maximum. That's why *I'm* testing this board instead of you. You're a walking definition of the engineering term 'test to destruction.'"

"Yeah, but how fast does it go?" Rick asked.

Tom sighed. "I don't have a speedometer on this thing, so you'll have to tell me. There's a radar gun—"

"Got it!" Rick said. "I'll just aim as you pass by and—" Rick's voice cut off with a loud gulp. "Um, would you believe, seventy-five?"

Tom was crouched on the board now, looking as though he were fighting a strong wind—and he was. Air resistance of more than seventy miles an hour was trying to tug him off the board.

"This is serious," Rick said. "When do I get my turn?"

"Serious?" Tom started to laugh. "It sure is . . . so why am I having such a good time?"

"Hey, don't let your dad know." Rick was laughing, too.

"No, we'll just give him the facts and figures," Tom said. "Like how this thing climbs."

Using the left-hand dial to throttle back the speed, Tom turned the right-hand dial. "Yeeaaah!" he yelled as the board went screaming into the sky.

"Tom!" Rick shouted. "Are you okay?"

"Yeah." Tom's voice was a little shaky as he answered. "Make a note for Dad. This thing climbs like a jet plane."

The skyboard was making a lazy circle, about a hundred feet in the air. Tom stared down. If he were a little higher, he could probably see Los Angeles. As it was, all of Central Hills was laid out at his feet.

Right below him, half-hidden in the hills, were the four square miles of Swift Enterprises. "You've got to hand it to Dad," Tom murmured. "When he designs something . . ."

The layout of the complex gave it the appearance of a small city, but the buildings themselves looked like a handful of jewels and bright metal that a giant had tossed into the mountain valley. The round dome of the fusion reactor gleamed in the center of the complex, reflecting in the glass-and-chrome faces of the lab buildings.

There was a lot of shining glass and pastel concrete, keeping the huge factory buildings light and cheerful. Below him, Tom saw the landing strips for planes and helicopters and the rocket launch site. Then came the parking lot for the three hundred Swift employees, and the brightly colored nursery that provided day care for their children.

But the center of his orbit was the testing fields. Even there, the usually grim concrete bunkers were built to fit into the colorful landscape.

Tom noticed that the area was filling up with people. The technicians at Swift Enterprises were used to seeing strange things. But an eighteen-year-old on a surfboard with ten stories of thin air under him—that got attention.

Tom quickly brought the skyboard down to the ground, kicked free of the straps, and went over to Rick. "Let's set up the maneuverability test." He bent over the operations console, his lean, handsome face turning slightly red. "I wish they wouldn't look at me."

"Hey, you're putting on quite a show," Rick told him. "Even if I don't understand how that crazy thing works."

"It's like the kid's trick of making a small magnet float over a bigger one," Tom told him. "Except, instead of a magnet, I'm using a superconductive ceramic."

"Get out of town! Ceramic, as in flowerpots?"

Tom laughed. "A little more heavy-duty than a flowerpot. This ceramic conducts electricity even better than copper wire. It has almost no resistance. And when it encounters a magnetic field, it acts like a mirror, reflecting itself away from the track." He shrugged. "The theory's been around for almost a century."

"But it took you to make it work." Rick shoved his hands into the back pockets of his worn jeans and shook his head. "No wonder those colleges like Harvard and MIT are willing to take you in right now."

Tom just winked. "But I like rooting for the Jefferson football team." He flicked a switch on the console and spoke into the microphone. "Robot! Do you hear me?"

"Receiving loud and clear." The robot sat in the center of the oval track, at a console that was a twin to the one Tom used. Around the robot a pattern of hatches was spread on the ground, making it look like a giant checkerboard.

"What are you supposed to be doing?" Rick's broad, good-natured face looked puzzled. "Playing chess?"

"Each square out there is a separate cell with a small but powerful electromagnet." Tom reached over to one side of the board and flicked some switches. "The trapdoors hide different, um, obstacles."

"What kind?" Rick asked.

Tom grinned. "Watch and see."

He hopped back on the skyboard, brought

it to humming life, and took off. This time, instead of going around the test track, he swept across it onto the checkerboard. "When I reach you, robot, the test is over."

"Understood." The robot's hands flew across the control console.

Instantly, a hatch on the ground opened, and a blast of compressed air tried to blow Tom off the board. Tom sent the board into a zigzag, avoiding the blasts.

"Some test, Swift," Rick needled Tom over his headphones. "It looks more like a giant fun house."

A hatch directly in front of Tom opened, and a jet of water burst out of a huge squirt gun. Grabbing the control knobs at his waist, Tom sent the board hurtling out of the line of fire.

Hatches were opening up all around the checkerboard, sending a wild assortment of "weapons" at Tom. Bags of flour, squirts of paint, and even a barrage of cream pies went into the air. Rick laughed at Tom's crazy sense of humor—cream pies! But Tom wove through the pattern of "fire" without being touched, like a hotdogger on an invisible wave.

"You're almost there," Rick said excitedly.

Tom brought the board around for a landing behind the control console. The robot swiveled its head, its photocell eyes gleaming.

Then its hand shot out to the power-grid controls, twisting a dial.

"Hey! You're not programmed to—"

That was as far as Tom got as the electromagnetic grid below him went crazy. The board bucked under his feet like an animal trying to toss him off.

Then it swooped into the air on a wild course, completely out of control. Tom struggled desperately, using the dials on his waist panel to straighten the skyboard out.

He'd almost succeeded when a random magnetic blast first jerked the board, then sent it tumbling. Tom's feet were knocked right out of the foot straps.

Then he was falling, with nothing below him but seventy feet of thin air—and the hard, cold ground.

2

TOM THREW OUT HIS ARMS LIKE A SKY DIVER, trying to slow his fall. "Rick—the air bags!" he yelled into his helmet mike. He was glad he'd thought to include the inflatable crash bags among his emergency equipment.

Big white patches blossomed on the ground as Rick triggered the air bags. The huge white sacks inflated in seconds. Technicians ran to help, pushing the bags together.

But Tom noticed that the robot at the control console had sprung into action. Tom couldn't figure what it was up to, but he knew plenty more dirty tricks were hidden under the hatches. They could foul up the rescue attempt. He brought his arms in, hastening his fall, so he could operate his own control panel.

9

A couple of twists at the dials and the skyboard rocketed through the now-stable magnetic fields. The board swooped down to catch the robot right in the head. Then, in a dazzling blast, the robot and the skyboard disappeared in an explosion.

Tom stared, astonished. He'd only meant to knock the robot down. But he had no time for further thoughts. The ground was coming up pretty quickly. Then the whole world turned white as Tom crashed into a mountain of inflated cushions.

The top air bag burst from the shock, but the rest of them cushioned Tom's fall. Rick scrambled up to him, shouting, "Tom! Are you okay?"

Tom lay spread-eagled in the pocket he'd made in the cushions. "I always wondered how a pin felt when it burst a balloon." Shaking his head, he hauled himself out of the collapsed air bag.

About a dozen Swift Enterprises employees—some from the emergency crew, others just technical staff—had gathered around. They looked up anxiously as Tom climbed down and removed his protective helmet and shoulder pads. "It's okay, everybody. I'm all right."

"What went wrong?" a young, dark-haired guy in a lab coat asked. "It looked like your test robot went out of control."

"Good thing you blew him up before he

really went to work on the controls," someone else said.

Tom shook his head. "I didn't mean to blow him up. Maybe I'll get a clue about what went wrong when I check out the wreckage."

"Good luck," the young guy said with a laugh.

Tom saw why. Robot parts were scattered all over the field, along with the smashed remains of the board. There weren't many pieces of skyboard—most of it had disintegrated into glowing powder. Tom saw only one major chunk, with one of the foot straps still attached.

Rick stared at the glittering debris. "What do we do with the, um, wreckage?"

"Clean it up with a broom, I guess." Tom scooped up a handful of glowing powder. Among the dust particles in his palm were sparking crystals that sent off tiny arcs of electricity wherever they touched one another or his skin. It was like looking at a microscopic lightning storm, or a minifireworks display—beautiful. But it didn't tell him what had gone wrong. None of his earlier tests had shown any possibility for the board's magnetic field disrupting computer brains. What other reason could there be?

Rick's voice cut into Tom's thoughts. "Ready for cleanup detail." He grinned as he marched onto the checkerboard with a large broom over his shoulder.

"Let's pick up all the stuff in this area. I want to study it." Tom let the sparking dust fall from his hand and looked for something to sweep the debris into.

He walked along the track, wondering if it could be the problem. Under the putty brown insulation was more of the special superconductor Tom had invented. When it was laid out in a circle, a revolving electrical charge caused magnetism. The magnetic field pushed against the superconductor in the board, making it float in the air.

Could the electromagnetic field also disrupt a robot's computer brain? If so, why weren't the simpler computer controls for the hatch doors affected?

Still mulling over the strange results, Tom carried a cardboard box back to where Rick was standing. His friend had swept up all the debris.

"We can probably load this into the back of my car," Rick began. Then he said, "Uh-oh, genius, what's on your mind now?"

"What are you talking about?" Tom asked.

"You have that don't-bother-me-I'm-inventing-something look on your face."

Tom had to laugh. He scratched his blond head, then said, "I was wondering how to shield computer chips from magnetism—and not having much luck." He loaded the gear from the failed experiment into the back of a fifteen-year-old red Jaguar XKE and hopped inside. Rick started the car's engine, which sounded more like a cement mixer than a speed machine.

"The timing's off on this old clunker," Tom said. "Why don't you let me under the hood—"

"Nobody touches my beautiful baby but me," Rick said, his hands on the wheel.

"Well, your beautiful baby sounds like it's about to throw up," Tom growled as they chugged toward the administration center. Yet he found himself smiling as he passed the buildings around him. The Central Hills complex was Tom's father's best invention—the perfect place for inventing. Freedom, equipment, and genius had been brought together to benefit the world. For Tom junior, it was part laboratory, part fantasyland, where anything he imagined could be made to work.

Well, almost anything. What had gone wrong with the test? The question gnawed at Tom as Rick continued driving down the road to the administration center. The glass-faced building was literally the center of Swift Enterprises. Every road in the complex branched out from there, like spokes in a wheel.

Rick pulled into a parking space, and Tom jumped out and removed the box full of debris from the rear. They headed across a wide lawn with shrubs and flowers, right for the main entrance.

Just inside was the receptionist's desk. Mary Ann Jennings looked up from her post. "Tom, your father wants to talk to you."

"I'm bringing this down to the lab. He can buzz me there in a few minutes," Tom said. "Or I'll go up to his office before I leave."

Tom and Rick crossed the huge lobby without even a glance at the old Swift rockets displayed on the walls. That was tourist stuff— though the "tourists" who came here were often brilliant scientists or world leaders. Beyond the main elevator bank, Tom stopped at an inconspicuous door and pushed a special data-key into a slot, calling up an elevator from the subbasement.

They got on and headed down. "This accident has really gotten to you," Rick said.

"I don't like things that don't make sense."

The elevator door opened onto a tiny room with a huge metal door facing them. The only decoration was the outline of a handprint, set in the center of the door. Tom stepped up and pressed his hand to it, making the print glow an eerie green. That meant the computerized door had recognized Tom. Only three handprints in the world would open the door— Tom's, his father's, and Rick's.

With a loud click, the door opened. Tom

and Rick headed down a long hallway, then headed left when two stairways branched off. Now they came to another door, this one with a speaker mounted in its middle. A mechanical voice boomed out, "Who recorded 'Hungry Like the Wolf'?"

Rick grinned and answered, "Duran Duran."

He shook his head as the door swung open. "I don't believe that you use rock trivia to guard your door. What happens if you can't answer a question?"

Tom shrugged. "Hasn't happened yet. Besides, the door is really checking for your voiceprint."

They stepped into Tom Swift's lab.

The room was the size of a basketball court, but partitions swung from the walls to make a barrier about ten feet from the door. In front of them stood a vaguely human shape—if humans were seven feet tall and made of shining metal.

"Hel-lo, Mas-ter," the robot droned in a loud metallic voice.

"What's the matter, Rob?" Rick asked. "Got a sore throat?"

"No, he just saw an old science-fiction movie last night," Tom said.

"*Vampires of the Ionosphere*," Rob said in a more normal voice. "Great flick. Watch."

The robot held up a videocassette, popped it into its chest, and turned toward a wall.

Beams of light shone from its head, forming a black-and-white picture on the wall. A robot made from old plumbing supplies marched stiffly along. "Kill-the-Earth-lings," it chanted in a tinny voice.

Rick stared, fascinated. "When did you install the VCR and projection TV into Rob?"

"I didn't," Tom said. "That's one of Orb's alterations." He looked around. "Speaking of which, where is your partner in crime?"

Rob clicked off the movie. "Orb had me carry him to Central Computing for a data share."

Rob and Orb had originally been designed as one robot, with a removable memory module. Orb was the data module, a basketball-size silvery sphere. Rob had started out as the delivery module, built to act as Orb's arms and legs. Tom's experiments with artificial intelligence had wound up with the two modules developing very different personalities. The robots had also made alterations to themselves.

"Open up the room and let's have some lights," Tom told Rob.

Immediately, the partitions slid into the walls as bright lights came on. The lab was filled with half-built—or half-disassembled—machines, scientific gear, and three computers. Two more boards like the one Tom had tested leaned against one wall. Another wall was filled with scientific graffiti—equations and diagrams, written in marker on a special washable paint.

Tom walked over to one of the worktables. "Give us some thinking music. I need to work something out."

Immediately, the music of an electric guitar began pulsing out of Rob's speakers. An amplifier in the corner picked up with the bass line, while another speaker thumped with drumbeats. "Who's the band, Rob?" Rick asked.

"Oh, it's just a little something I've been working up," the robot answered.

Tom dumped the wreckage on a lab table and began going through it.

"Come on, Tom, don't let it get to you," Rick said, going to a large box in the corner. On one side Tom had spray-painted the word *OOPS* in large red letters. "Let's see what other items rated F for Failure we have in here."

After rummaging for a second, he came up with a sealed carton. "Aha! Remember these?"

Rick opened the box, and the air filled with buzzing—a high, whiny hum.

Tom turned from his work. "You didn't let the robot pollinators loose?"

Tiny little winged robots now zoomed around the room. Tom had designed them to pollinate plants, but their tiny electronic brains recognized almost anything as plant-like. They had tried to pollinate clothing, people's ears, people's noses. Not only was their buzzing more annoying than a mosquito's, they were harder to swat.

"So what do you think went wrong today?" Rick asked.

"Maybe I can find out by duplicating the test here in the lab." Tom cleared a space on the table, then picked up a spray can. "This is phase two of the board project. Maglev—magnetic levitation—is what keeps the board in the air. But it needs an electromagnet underneath it, sort of like a train needs rails. Believe it or not, this can contains spray-on rails."

"What do you mean?" Rick asked.

"Seeing is believing." Tom aimed the can at the cleared section of the table and sprayed, leaving a brownish tan oval. "What did I just do?"

"Ruined the tabletop?" Rick suggested.

"I've just laid down an electromagnet," Tom said, tapping the now-dry ring. "It's an ultrathin layer of my superconductor between two layers of insulation."

"I still don't understand this superconductor thing," Rick said. "I thought it worked only at hundreds of degrees below zero."

"That's right," Tom said. "Mixtures like Paul Chu's yttrium ceramic work only under intense cold. But I was able to add my own wrinkle to the formula—solid electricity."

He held up a glass jar full of glowing dust. "Each of these points of light is a long, thin, tiny crystal. The molecules that build up these crystals each have another molecule inside. You see, trapped within a lattice of carbon atoms—"

"Tom, you've lost me," Rick said.

"Okay, I'll make it simple. When these crystals form, they trap an electrical charge inside. They're like one-cell superconductors. And when they're baked into Chu's Compound One-Two-Three, they make it a lot more useful."

"Not too useful, if it drives robots crazy," Rick said.

"I don't think the materials were the problem. Watch." Tom opened the jar of crystals and poured some over his electromagnet oval.

Rick stared as the glowing crystals floated in midair over the magnetic field, like a halo. "This looks familiar," he said.

"Now all we need are some robots." Tom began shooing the little pollinators toward his experiment. As soon as they saw the glowing circle, they thought it was a flower. Immediately, the air over the electromagnet was buzzing with the little creatures.

"They don't seem to be going nuts," Tom said.

"Maybe they don't have enough brains to be affected," Rick suggested.

"That's a point." Tom began digging through the wreckage again. "If only I could find some pieces of the robot's computer brain. But it's the top half of him that blew up."

Tom waved his hands to keep several of the mechanical bugs from pollinating his face. Several more crept into the robot leg he was examining.

He shook the leg to get them out, and something fell onto the table.

Tom looked at the item so intently, he ignored the cloud of robot bugs flying around his face.

"Find something?" Rick asked, swatting at a passing pollinator.

"Maybe," Tom said thoughtfully. "It's a piece of circuit board, with what looks like a memory chip—pretty badly burned."

"Robot legs have memory?"

Tom shrugged. "It was inside there, but is it from the robot or the board?" He tapped the little fragment, frowning. "Whatever it is, it doesn't look like standard Swift equipment."

He glanced at Rick. "So what was it doing on our testing grounds?"

3

THIS WAS USED TO SABOTAGE THE TEST?" RICK stared at the fragment of computer equipment.

"Maybe," Tom said. "Superconductivity is hot science these days. Maybe someone doesn't want my skyboard to—"

"Tom," a deep voice spoke behind them. Both boys whirled to see Tom's father standing in the middle of the lab. Rob instantly cut the music.

Tom Swift, Sr.'s blond hair was streaked with gray, and his face had lines that would soon become wrinkles. But his piercing blue eyes were as sharp and as young as his son's. He seemed nearly transparent—and the boys realized that he was! They were facing a transmitted hologram.

"I patched into the test cameras to follow

your experiment this morning." Mr. Swift's handsome face was set in a frown. "What happened?"

"The robot on the control console went berserk," Tom said.

"Tom thinks—" Rick began, but Tom motioned behind his back to shut him up.

"It needs more work," Tom said. A tiny robot bug crawled into his ear. Tom rubbed vigorously, trying to dislodge the little pollinator.

Mr. Swift sighed. "I don't tell you what to research, Tom. But Swift Enterprises is depending on you for this superconductor."

The ghostly figure looked serious. "Superconductive cables would make the power grid so efficient that we'd save sixty power stations' worth of fuel. What are your cost projections? Have you started work on them yet?"

"Uh—no."

"I know you're interested in maglev—so are lots of people. But what can we show them? Our frictionless vehicle is a flying surfboard."

He shook his head. "Your skyboard is an expensive project—just look what this last test has cost us. So far, we've paid for it out of the general fund for superconductivity. Unless you start getting results, we'll have to start taking the costs out of *your* lab budget."

Now it was Tom's turn to sigh. "I see."

"So do me a favor, and clear out the bugs."
Mr. Swift smiled, and his image slowly faded.

"I wonder if he meant that literally." Rick
swatted a pollinator, then got more serious.
"Why didn't you say the test was sabotaged?"

"There's no proof—and I wouldn't give Dad
an excuse like that unless I could back it up.
He's got a lot on his mind these days."

"So what do we do now?"

"I don't know about you, but *I've* got a
bunch of cost projections to come up with,"
Tom said.

"We were heading for the beach today,
remember?" Rick asked. "Sandra said lots of
people would be there." He glanced slyly at
Tom. "And I hear Dan Coster's cousin Mandy
is supposed to be going along."

"Mandy Coster will be there?" Tom spoke
eagerly, until he saw his friend's smug grin.
"I mean, uh, good. Nice chance for her to
meet people, since she just moved to Central
Hills."

"Nice chance for her to know *you* better,"
Rick said, rubbing in his discovery that Tom
liked Mandy.

Tom couldn't help the grin that spread over
his face. "Come to think of it, you're right."

"All work and no play . . ." Rick went on.

"Hey, I'm convinced. But I've got to get the
projections started. Rob"—Tom turned to the
robot—"get Orb on the hologram."

In seconds, another ghostly figure appeared. This one was much smaller—a basketball-size silver sphere sitting on the floor.

"You need to speak to me, Tom?" Orb's voice was always quiet, always polite, but somehow robotlike. It sounded as if Orb had been pulled away from deep thoughts.

"I need computer projections," Tom said. "Costs versus benefits for using my superconductor for power cables. You know—materials, manufacturing, how much money we'd have to make to break even, against the energy savings."

"There are a number of variables to deal with," Orb said. "It should be ready by four o'clock this afternoon."

Tom grinned. "Great. I'll check with you then." He turned to Rob. "Helping Orb is now your top priority. If anyone else gives you a job, tell them that I've assigned you to help Orb."

"Got it," Rob said. "Orb shouldn't need much. He's already in the computer center."

Orb hesitated for a second. "Correct. But I am glad to have first call on Rob." The image of the ball winked out of existence.

"Go have fun," Rob told Tom. "I'm not a beach person myself—hate getting sand in my gears. Orb and I will take care of those projections." He tapped a finger on his metal chest.

24

"After all, why invent labor-saving devices if you don't use us to save labor?"

In spite of Rob's words, Tom wasn't exactly happy as he and Rick drove out the main gate in Rick's rumbling XKE.

"Hey, worrying about those projections won't get them done any faster," Rick said. "As for the other stuff your father said—" He shrugged. "Well, you wanted something small and portable to test this magnetic levitation thing. Building a flying car would have been a lot more expensive."

"Yeah, but a flying model train would have been a lot easier, smaller, and cheaper."

"A model couldn't take a person up," Rick pointed out.

"That was my argument for building the board," Tom said. "Now I wonder if I was just showing off." He grinned. "After all, a flying surfboard is pretty cool."

They drove through quiet, brown hills, but at the new Central Mall, the desert ended and southern California began. Gaudy colors glared from all directions as they joined the traffic creeping past fast-food joints, car lots, and shopping centers.

"Just think—if you really get this maglev thing going, we could fly over all these cars." Rick sighed as he stared at the traffic.

"If it really got going, we'd probably just have flying traffic jams," Tom said with a grin.

They came to a section of old adobe mission-style buildings. This was the original Central Hills business district—from before the high-tech invasion of Swift Enterprises. Rick turned off the main road. "Let's stop off at my house and pick up some bathing suits."

After a two-minute stop at the Cantwells', the boys were on the road again, heading for the beach. Even with miles of Pacific coastline to choose from, "the beach" meant only one place—Laguna Pequeña. The small bay off the ocean offered the best swimming and sand around.

"How do we find Sandra in this mob?" Tom stared at the packed beach as they pulled up to park.

"Well, there's her Firebird," Rick said. "And your little sister made it easy on us." He reached into his pocket and pulled out a box about the size of a cigarette pack. Flicking a switch, he waved the box back and forth until it gave off a loud *ping*. "This way," Rick said.

"That's a Swift homing device," Tom said. "How did you—"

"Sandra gave it to me—she's holding the other end," Rick said, leading the way.

Tom laughed. "So Sandra's running a high-tech romance. I'll have to remember that trick."

"Just get a girlfriend first," Rick teased.

They threaded their way through the crowd

to an empty beach blanket. The pinging got louder and louder as Rick approached Sandra's beach bag.

"Hey, Rick, you didn't expect her to go swimming with that gizmo, did you?" asked a soft female voice behind them.

They turned to see Mandy Coster, her dark brown eyes sparkling with laughter. She had obviously just come out of the water and was smoothing back her long, wet chestnut hair. A red bathing suit showed off her trim figure and a nice tan.

"Come on, I'll lead you to her." Mandy turned and headed for the water again.

Rick tossed the homer on the blanket with a laugh. "So much for technology."

They followed Mandy into the water and found Sandra and Dan out in the surf. Sandra's blond hair made a brilliant contrast to her bright blue suit. She turned at Mandy's call. "Hey, Sandra, those guys are here!"

"Yo, Tom-Tom!" Dan Coster shook water out of his long, curly black hair. "Whatcha say?"

"I hear the Scavengers are playing at Freddie's," Tom said, naming a favorite local club. "Your band is going places."

"It'll be a great gig." Dan struck a chord on an imaginary guitar. "I'll have more babe trouble than ever."

A gorgeous blonde spread out her beach

blanket near the water. "Whoa," Dan muttered. "This is someone I've got to meet."

He dashed out of the surf and straight to the girl. "Hey, babe, there are two choices here. We could go swimming together, or I could rub tanning oil on that lovely bod." He flashed her a wide smile.

Tom couldn't believe Dan's nerve. And he really couldn't believe it when the girl smiled up at his friend. He moved closer to hear what she'd say.

"You forgot the third choice," the girl cooed. "You could go swimming out alone—and never come back."

Then she turned her back on Dan, who just shrugged and returned to his friends in the surf.

"I don't believe you, Dan Coster," Sandra Swift said.

"Hey, you don't expect me to hit on you with your brother and your boyfriend here?"

Sandra glared at him. "No. I expect you to just . . . cool off!"

She spun her arms, splashing Dan and starting a general water fight. Rick took the windmill approach, throwing water everywhere. Tom was a sniper, kneeling in the surf and squirting water from his cupped hands. He could direct a deadly accurate stream up to ten feet, as Dan Coster discovered when he got zapped.

"How'd you do that?" Mandy said. She cupped her hands—and squirted herself in the eye.

"It, uh, takes a little practice," Tom said, looking at Mandy's dripping face.

"I'll stick with the old-fashioned way." Mandy turned away, scooping a handful of water to throw. Tom sighed. She'd been interested, and he'd blown it.

"Okay, now we're all wet. How about a swim?" Rick hollered. It soon turned into a race, with Rick churning in the lead. At last, they headed back to the beach blanket to dry off.

"So how'd the experiment go this morning?" Sandra asked Tom.

He shrugged. "Well—"

"The robot testing the board went bonkers and tried to send Tom into orbit," Rick said. "Tom got flung loose and broke an air bag when he landed."

"Thanks, Rick," Tom muttered sourly, until he noticed Mandy's concerned look.

"A flying surfboard?" Mandy stared at Tom.

"It's just an experiment in maglev—uh, magnetic levitation. That's, uh—" Tom felt his face going red. Why couldn't he talk normally around Mandy?

"It's a special surfboard that floats over a huge electromagnet," Rick translated.

Tom tried again. "See, I've been working on superconductors—"

"Superconductors? You mean the guys in the Tokyo subways who push extra passengers into the trains?" Dan grinned as he ran a towel over his hair.

Rick groaned as he flopped on the blanket. "It's no joke, Dan." He suddenly sat up. "Hey, Tom, why not give them a demonstration? You have two boards left."

Tom shook his head. "I don't think—"

Rick grinned eagerly. "No robots around. Just you and me, away from the complex. It would give you a chance to test that superconductor spray."

"Where would we do it?" Tom asked.

"Right here!" Sandra exclaimed. "We'll have a beach party and demonstration."

Rick and Sandra looked at each other, their eyes glowing with excitement. He's just doing this to show off for her, Tom said to himself.

Mandy Coster came up close, laying her hand on his arm. "You'll really fly?" she asked.

Tom nodded. He wasn't above showing off a little himself. "Okay, let's do it."

"Way to go, Swift," Mandy said, throwing an arm around him.

Tom felt great—until he remembered the cost projections. "I've got work to do at my lab. Sorry, but I'll have to cut out."

"Take my car." Sandra dug the keys out of her bag. "I'll get a lift home with Rick."

Climbing into Sandra's Firebird, Tom realized he'd be back at the lab well before the deadline he'd set for Orb. He picked up the car phone, dialed the Swift complex, then hit the special code that contacted Orb.

"Orb here," the robot's voice came over the line.

"I'll be back early," Tom said. "Expect me at the lab in about half an hour. You can start feeding me the projections then."

"The projections should be ready," Orb said. "I'll transmit them from here in the computer center and have Rob print them out."

As Orb spoke, Tom heard a faint noise in the background. "What was that?" he asked.

"What?"

"Forget it, Orb." Tom hung up. He started the car, shaking his head. "Must be hearing things," he muttered.

Orb had told him he was in the computer center. But Tom could swear he'd heard the buzz of a high-security checkpoint in the background.

That was impossible. Those checkpoints were located around places like the explosives lab, not the data center.

TOM STOPPED HIS CAR RIGHT BY THE SWIFT Enterprises gate and broke into laughter. "You don't usually see the chief of security pulling duty at the front door," he said, grinning. "What happened, Harlan? Did you lose a bet?"

"Oh, I take it on every once in a while, just to keep me humble." Harlan Ames cracked a smile in a face so deeply tanned it looked like leather. His white hair and weather-beaten skin might say "old man," but his lean blue-uniformed form strode to the convertible with the walk of a man half his age.

"I heard about your show this morning. Would have been pretty impressive, if your robot hadn't gone haywire." Ames's voice lowered. "Or *did* it just go haywire?"

Tom gave him a startled look. "What makes you say that?"

"A lot of things—like the way you just clammed up on me." Ames's voice stayed low. "Your dad's been quietly beefing up our security. He's done it gradually over the last few months, bringing in more men—and lots more hardware."

Ames frowned. "You know, I've worked for your dad since he started this company. We've gone through some hairy times together. So if he's worried about something, I'd take it very seriously."

His frown deepened. "I'd love to know what's going on—especially if I'm supposed to run security around here."

Tom shook his head. "I wish I could tell you, Harlan. This is all news to me."

"Well, I haven't been sitting behind my desk, waiting to be told," Ames said. "I've done a little investigating."

"Find anything?"

Ames shrugged. "Lots of things—most with no connection to this red alert." He grinned. "You know your pal Rick is getting free samples of some Swift prototypes? Too bad your sister doesn't give him an automatic engine tuner."

Tom had to laugh. "I just found out today. Maybe I'll invent one for Sandra to give him."

"Now for an unfunny question. Where's

that kid at the Bomb Palace getting the extra money he's spreading around?" The Bomb Palace was the company's nickname for the Explosive Compounds Lab. Built like a fortress, even Mr. Swift's design genius couldn't tone down the place's grimness.

"Who's that?" Tom asked.

"Garret Frayne, a young programmer down there. Nowadays they blow things up on computers—you know, simulations. I suppose it's better than blowing the roof off. Your father did that once, when we were back in Lake Carlopa."

The mention of computers reminded Tom that he was supposed to be at work.

"Harlan, I'd love to hear that story—it might come in handy when Dad gets on my case. I've been working on something you might like for your night patrols, too."

Ames laughed. "Well, you know where to find me, at least until five o'clock."

Tom drove to the administration center, then headed down to his lab. Rob stood by the door, a pile of computer printouts in his arms.

"How about some music, Rob? A fast beat to help get through this stuff quickly."

The speakers immediately began pouring a rhythmic instrumental number.

"And, Rob—" Tom handed the robot a scribbled list. "Can you collect this gear? I need it for this evening. We're trying a night-time skyboard test on the beach."

Rob's photocell "eyes" glowed as he looked over the list. "Most of this stuff is around here," he said. "As for the rest, well, I've got time to build it." He marched off.

Tom spent the rest of the afternoon doing business math. "Hey, Rob," he asked as he wrote some suggestions on one page. "Where's Orb?"

The robot looked up from the worktable where he was assembling some equipment. His eyes glowed for a second, then dimmed. "Still at the computer center, I guess. Want me to call him?"

Tom shook his head. "I took him off whatever he was doing to help me out. Let him finish, and then we'll polish up these projections."

Tom continued working until six o'clock, when Rob gently tapped him on the shoulder. "You told me to remind you when it was—"

His voice was cut off by the telephone. Rick's voice came out of the speaker. "I was afraid you'd get hypnotized by those numbers and forget about this evening," he said. "We're supposed to hit the beach in an hour."

"Rob just reminded me of the time," Tom said.

"So? Are we ready?"

Tom looked to Rob. "Are we ready?"

The robot swept an arm over the pile of equipment Tom had asked for. "I don't know if you're ready, but I have everything you asked for."

"Do we need *all* this stuff?" Rick puffed as they carried a load from Tom's rolling lab to the hard-packed sand on the beach. Dan Coster had helped a little, then drifted back to the bonfire, where most of the kids were hanging out.

Rick wistfully sniffed the delicious smells of cooking food. "Boy, when your sister sets up a cookout, she doesn't fool around."

"Mmmm. I wonder if she brought our laser hot-dog cooker?" Tom screwed a spray attachment onto a can of his liquid superconductor.

"I didn't know you'd come up with a laser hot-dog . . ." Rick's voice died away. "I walked right into that one, didn't I?"

Tom grinned at him. "Go get some food. I'm ready to test the spray."

He walked along the beach, laying down a thin coat of superconductor on the sand.

"I don't believe this!" Mandy, in jeans and a pink sweater, came to stare at Tom's work. "It looks like you're spraying a carpet of stars on the sand." In the darkness, the solid electricity crystals sparkled through the thin insulation.

She walked along the glowing track with Tom, her eyes shining. Her long chestnut hair hung in little curls around her shoulders. "This is hot, Swift," she said. "I really mean it."

"Yeah," Tom echoed. "Really hot."

Mandy glanced over and realized that Tom was looking at her. Her head went down, and she fiddled with her gold chain.

They walked a little farther along the growing track. Come on, Tom told himself. What would Rick do? What would Dan do? No—change that thought. I don't want to scare her off.

Finally, he cleared his throat and spoke. "I just hope the spray works as well as it looks. This is our first test." He glanced over at Mandy. "And I'm glad you came over to check things out."

"Oh?" She stepped away a little. "I thought you'd be too busy to stop by the party—just like you had to go and work this afternoon."

How could he answer that? "Look, Mandy, I've got a lot of stuff going down right now, and—"

"You don't have time for new things in your life?" Mandy turned away, biting her lip.

"I mean, it's not easy to do all the things I'd like." Tom held out the sprayer attachment. "Want to spray stars for a while?"

She grinned at him, then set her face in a look of extravagant suspicion. "Are you setting me up to squirt myself again?"

"No way. There's a fifty-fifty chance that *I* could be the target," Tom told her.

They finished spraying the racetrack together in silence. Mandy headed off for the bonfire as Rick came back, hot dog in one hand, hamburger in the other.

"So how'd it go?" he said, taking a bite of his burger.

"I've got the track laid down. Next, we—"

"I mean with Mandy," Rick said.

Tom sighed. "I don't know. She didn't seem too interested right now. But this afternoon—"

"This afternoon, you ran off on her," Rick said. "You don't have to be a genius to see that she might think *you* weren't interested."

Tom looked at his friend. "I'm not very good at this. It's not like working in a lab. Mix two chemicals, and I know how they'll react. But I can't tell you how girls react."

"Well, you just have to experiment," Rick told him. "Besides, I wouldn't give up hope. After all, she came out to see you."

Tom brightened as he unwrapped the two skyboards—one red, one blue. Rick laid out the control panels, helmets and pads, and a pair of shiny white jackets.

"You think of everything, Swift," he said, "even racing jackets." He held one up. "But couldn't you come up with something a little more stylish? Like black leather? This is kind of bulky, and it comes down below my hips."

"It's for safety, not fashion," Tom said. "There's a little ring up by the neck piece. If you get into any trouble on the board, yank it."

"And?" Rick said.

"And a dynasail comes out," Tom told him. "It fills with compressed air in about three seconds and is totally maneuverable. Rob put it together, based on some doodles I'd done."

Rick shook his head. "Let's hope we don't have to test *that*."

A crowd of kids came from the bonfires to marvel at the glowing track. Sandra came, too, carrying a plate heaped with hamburgers. "Some supplies for your trip," she said, a grin on her pretty face.

"Mmm, delicious." Rick grabbed another burger and started eating.

"How about you, Tom?" Mandy asked.

"I'll have just one." Tom glanced at Rick. "Got to keep my racing weight down." He grinned as Rick nearly choked.

Pulling a cable he'd run from the van he used as a mobile lab, Tom hooked it up to the now-dry superconductor spray. "We'll let it charge up while we get into our gear."

Rick slipped into the padding and jacket but stared at the helmet. "I can understand the mike and earphones, but I wouldn't think you'd need a tinted visor for night flying."

Tom grinned as he pulled on his own equipment. "Try it."

Rick put the helmet on. "I still don't see—" he began, slipping the visor down. "But I do now!"

Tom pulled down his visor—and the darkness around him disappeared. He could see everything clearly, but it looked like the landscape of another planet. The beach and the hills beyond were all tinted red, and the people around him glowed slightly. A brilliant band of color tinged the sky in the west, where the sun had set. The flame of the bonfire was blinding.

"Night vision!" Rick exclaimed.

"Ruby-lensed infrared visors," Tom said. "They actually read heat waves—the warmer the object, the brighter the light. I'm making some glasses for Harlan Ames's people."

"Great. Well, I'm ready to go." Rick grabbed a board and headed for the track.

"This spray-on film isn't as strong as the other track," Tom warned. "We'll probably go up only a couple of feet—if we go up at all."

"Just one way to find out," Rick said, clamping his feet into the foot straps.

Tom tested the radio link with Rick and with his sister, who stood at the mobile lab's control board. "Sandra," he said into his mike, "everything ready?"

"Looks good from here," she said. "I'll move in with remote control if anything goes wrong."

"Okay, then." Tom clamped on his own straps. "Let's go for it!"

He and Rick moved the height controls. The boards floated into the air, bringing gasps from the kids. Tom could hear Dan Coster's yell of "Outrageous!"

"How's it feel?" Tom asked Rick.

"A little wobbly," his friend replied.

"The spray must be a little uneven so the magnetic field is uneven, too." Tom didn't mind the feeling. He felt as if he were bobbing on water. "Let's try once around the track," he said, "just to get the feel of it."

"Okay," Rick responded. "Then, when we come past Sandra, we'll speed it up."

His hand went to the speed control, and Tom followed. Their movement was more choppy than smooth, but they could handle it. Upping the speed helped.

As they passed Sandra, Rick really poured it on. He whipped ahead of Tom, who sped up to pull even with him again.

"How about a little race?" Rick asked. Tom couldn't see Rick's face through the visor, but he knew his friend was grinning a challenge at him.

"Okay. But keep it under seventy— Hey!"

Rick shot off again, with Tom zooming in pursuit. The slight roughness of the ride made the race more exciting. Instead of floating easily, Tom felt as if he were on the crest of a monster wave of energy, always on the brink of falling. The wind pulled at him as he upped his speed again.

Five feet ahead, Rick bent to cut his air resistance. Tom crouched a little lower, cutting his own wind profile. The clump of spectators passed in a blur.

"Hey, guys," Sandra's voice cut in over their earphones. "We just clocked you doing ninety!"

Tom moved to slow down, but Rick just whooped and sped up. Then they were suddenly swooping up, gaining altitude at an incredible rate. "What the—?" Tom yelled, fighting his controls.

"You're not responding to remote control." Sandra's voice sounded scared.

"Tom—we've left the track!" Rick yelled. They still swept on, controlled by another magnetic field.

"Time to bail out," Tom said, tearing loose from the foot straps. He grabbed the ring on his jacket, pulled, and felt the dynasail fill and expand. He maneuvered it easily down to the beach.

But when he looked for Rick's dynasail,

Tom saw him still crouched over his board. "Forget about it," Tom said. "Get off now!"

"I—I can't!" Rick's voice was tight. "My foot strap is stuck."

A tight, cold fist squeezed Tom's stomach as he watched his friend leave the magnetic field and start tumbling to the ground. "Rick!" he yelled.

A black shape came whispering out of the sky. Through his infrared visor, Tom recognized the shape of an attack helicopter, painted and modified for a stealth mission.

The chopper dropped like a striking hawk for Rick and his board, a net flying out to catch both in midair.

As Tom stared, the dark intruder changed course, heading up and east while it drew his netted friend inside.

5

TOM WAS IMMEDIATELY UP AND RUNNING. HE tore off his dynasail, tossing it behind him as he dashed for the mobile lab.

"Where's Rick? What's happened to him?" Sandra cried as he passed her.

"He's been kidnapped."

Sandra stared. "Kidnapped? How—who?"

"Right now, the big question is *where*." Tom lunged past her, through the back door of the van. He punched the power button on one of the pieces of equipment inside. A small screen lit up, showing a fast-moving blip of green light. "Let's see if we can track them on the radar."

Even as they looked, the blip began to get fuzzy. "They've got very good stealth equipment on board," Tom said grimly. "We're losing the signal."

"What are we going to do?" Sandra asked.

Tom snatched up the mobile phone and punched in a number. "I'm going to try to patch us into NORAD. The air force should be able to tell where this guy is heading." Tom scowled as he kept hitting buttons. "These stupid security codes. Ah—got it!"

The little screen before them took on a clearer definition as the government's radar system began feeding it information.

"They're headed due east—straight into the Sierra Nevada," Sandra said, her face pale. "If they land somewhere in those mountains, we'll have a tough time finding—"

Tom turned to his sister. "Get on the phone in your car and call Dad. Tell him what's happened. He can start organizing a rescue team. Besides, it wouldn't hurt to have another fix on this chopper."

The mystery helicopter's stealth gear was giving even the Defense Department's hardware a tough time. Tom watched tight-lipped as the blip went fuzzy again.

Dan Coster stuck his head in the back of the van. "Yo, Tom." His voice was serious— no "Tom-Tom" banter now. "Is there anything Mandy and I can do?" he asked.

"Organize a search," Tom said. "Somehow or other, these guys managed to plant a pretty powerful electromagnet at the end of our racing track. Only a conflicting magnetic field could make us fly off like that." He thought for a second. "Maybe it's in those rocks over by—"

His voice was cut off by a thunderous explosion nearby. Dan glanced back from the van. "It came from those rocks you were just talking about."

Tom sighed. "Blowing up the evidence."

"Well, we don't know if those guys did it right," Dan said. He turned to Mandy. "Come on, let's check for pieces."

Sandra Swift reappeared in the open door. "Dad's on-line with NORAD, too—he says they're losing the chopper!" Her eyes were swimming with unshed tears.

Tom didn't need her to give him the bad news. He stared bitterly at the radarscope, watching the blip on the screen spread out and disappear. "They've probably landed. And at least we've got a reasonable idea of where to search, even if it is a lot of territory."

He swung down out of the rear of the van. "We can't help Rick from here anymore. Let's head back to the complex."

He called to Dan and Mandy. They came hustling back, carrying a few pieces of blasted equipment.

"The stuff there was pretty much zapped,"

Dan said. "These were about the biggest pieces."

"Toss them in the back of the van," Tom said. "We're out of here."

"What about your other stuff?" Mandy asked, pointing at the control setup and the track. "And your board is out there somewhere."

"Leave it. We'll pick it up later," Tom said. "Right now, I want to see what Dad intends to do."

The small parade of cars that followed Tom's van joined a bigger parade at the gates of the Swift Enterprises complex. The whole place was a beehive of activity, with cars and trucks coming and going. Standing in the gates with a squad of security people was Harlan Ames.

"Nobody gets in unless they're vouched for," Ames told Tom when he pulled up.

"They're all eyewitnesses to Rick's kidnapping," Tom said.

Ames nodded. "Like the man said, 'The game's afoot.' And it looks like our team can use all the help it can get." He waved Tom and the others in. "Your father is waiting to see you."

They headed for the administration building, parked, and went up to Mr. Swift's office. Tom's father was seated behind his desk, handling about four calls at once on the speakerphone.

One wall of the office was taken up with a holographic aerial view of the Sierra Nevada mountains. Tom watched as the image zoomed in until only the area where the helicopter had disappeared was on the wall.

Mr. Swift completed his business, then looked grimly at the kids. "I want to hear exactly what happened tonight."

Tom led off, explaining about the test of the superconductor spray and the boards. The others chipped in with various details, leading up to the two boards taking off into the sky. Then Tom described the helicopter.

"I think someone set up a powerful electromagnet near the place where we were testing," Tom finished. "That's what made the boards go out of control."

"Something was hidden in some rocks near the track, but it blew up." Dan gestured to the cardboard box he held under one arm. "We've got some pieces in here."

"I'll have our lab people examine them and see what they can find out," Mr. Swift said, pressing a call button on the phone. Then he turned back to Tom, his face set in strained lines. "I've already spoken to the Cantwell family. If anything happens to Rick—"

"It's my fault." Tom finished the sentence as everyone stared at him. "I knew that something weird was going on with the boards, and I should never have taken them out of the complex for a test. But I thought that no one would know what we were doing."

"Then either you were followed—or we have a very good spy in this complex. And I already know the answer to that one." Mr. Swift sagged back in his seat. "It's not your fault, Tom. It's mine. I should have warned you and Sandra about some of the things that have been going on lately."

"Like what?" Sandra wanted to know.

"Industrial espionage, to start," Mr. Swift said. "A couple of months ago, I ran a computer search to find the perfect people to head two new projects. But before I even spoke to them, they both mysteriously got new jobs and disappeared. It's as if someone found out exactly what we were going to work on and then stepped in to foul us up. When the only major supply of silane in the country blew up, wrecking another project, I realized that's exactly what was going on."

He shook his head. "The lucky thing is that the spy has sent only *information* about what we're working on. He hasn't been able to smuggle actual working models or prototypes out of the complex. But then, we haven't been able to find this person."

"So that's why you've been quietly beefing up security," Tom said.

Mr. Swift looked up in surprise.

"Harlan Ames mentioned it to me today. He wanted to know what was going on," Tom explained. "He's also been doing some investigating. Apparently, somebody down in the Bomb Palace has been spending a lot of unexplained extra cash."

"What's the person's name?" Sandra demanded.

"Garret Frayne," Tom said. "He works in the computer simulations department."

"I'm going to check out Frayne's office." Sandra headed for the door. "If he doesn't know we suspect him, there may be clues to tell us who he's working for—and where they've taken Rick."

It was an unrealistic hope, but after one look at her determined face, neither Tom nor his father raised an objection. Sandra walked out of the room.

"Maybe we should catch up with this Frayne guy and keep an eye on him," Dan suggested.

"That'll be my job," Mandy said. "I'm new in town. He won't recognize me."

When Tom looked as if he was about to object, she said, "Hey, I'm not going to arrest him or anything. I'll just find out where he is and call you with the information."

Mr. Swift hit the keyboard on his desk, and another wall disappeared to show Frayne's personnel record. Tom stared at the hologram display of Frayne's face—a face that seemed familiar.

"Wait a second. I've seen him before." He stared at Frayne's handsome young face and jet black hair. "He was out on the testing field this afternoon, by the air bags, when Rick and I landed."

Tom stood in front of the image, frowning. "He was wearing a lab coat, and he even talked to me. But if he's in computer simulations, what was he doing out there?"

"While you try to come up with answers, I'll see if I can find him," Mandy said. She walked around the image, studying it carefully. Then she stepped out of the office, to get on the elevator outside.

"Be careful," Tom called after her.

"I've got a job for you, Tom," his father said. "And maybe your friends can help you with it. We're taking the Rover out of mothballs to search for Rick. You'll supervise getting it ready. I want it in the air over the Sierra Nevada at first light tomorrow—"

The ringing of a phone interrupted him. Mr. Swift picked up the receiver. "What is it? Oh, Nordstrum, you've looked over that blown-up debris I sent to the lab. What have you found out?"

Tom's father listened for a moment, his eyes going wide with disbelief. Stabbing the speakerphone button, he said, "Could you repeat that, please?"

Nordstrum's voice filled the whole office. "As you suspected, sir, the pieces seem to come from an electromagnet. But the strange thing is what the magnet was made from. It all seems to be old-fashioned Swift Enterprises equipment."

"Thank you, Nordstrum. Keep looking and see what else you can find." Mr. Swift cut the connection. "This keeps striking closer and closer to home."

The office suddenly rocked with enough force to crack the windows and throw Dan to one knee.

"What's going on?" he asked. "An earthquake?"

"An explosion." Tom's father rushed to the broad window panel. His face went white.

"An explosion in the Bomb Palace!"

6

Tom's father moved from the window to the door as if he'd been shot from a cannon. "Sandra was heading over there. She's probably in Frayne's office by now."

The phones on his desk were ringing and flashing like a light show. Mr. Swift ignored them, dashing out the office door. "I'm going to the Bomb Palace," he told his secretary. "If people want to report to me about what's going on, they can report to me there."

Dan followed Mr. Swift, but Tom held back, grabbing a phone on the secretary's desk.

"What are you doing, Tom?" Mr. Swift asked, turning from the elevator.

"Getting some extra help," Tom replied. He quickly dialed a number and said, "Meet me in the lobby—right away."

When they arrived downstairs, they saw immediately whom Tom had called. Rob stood gleaming beside the reception desk. The guard who sat behind it stared at the robot, a little bit in awe. "Uh, Mr. Swift," the guard said, "a car should be here in a moment. . . ."

"Forget that," Tom said, "I've got a van right outside."

They piled into the van and headed down the avenue that led to the Bomb Palace. Fire fighting and rescue trucks were already there, and so were security guards trying to keep the area clear of night-shift workers.

"Turn off there! Let the more important traffic through!" one young guard yelled at Tom. He nearly swallowed his whistle when he recognized the man in the passenger's seat. "Mr. Swift?"

The guard quickly cleared a path for them. Soon they were on the front lines of the damage-control struggle. The Bomb Palace didn't look like a fortress anymore. At least two of the top floors had caved in, and an ugly crack straggled across the building's concrete facade.

"It'll be dangerous going in there," Harlan Ames said to Mr. Swift. "Luckily no one was inside at this time of night."

"I have reason to believe someone *is* in there." Mr. Swift's voice was hollow. "My daughter was going to Garret Frayne's office."

Ames's eyes went to the ruined upper stories of the structure. "That's on the third floor from the top, here toward the front," he said. "It may be—"

Mr. Swift's face looked determined as he cut him off. "Get me a map. I'm going in."

Ames looked at Tom's father for a moment, but he knew better than to argue at a time like this. It was very clear. Mr. Swift was ready to risk his own life to save his daughter. "All right, sir, but I'm going in, too."

"Me, too," said Tom.

"Think I'm going to miss this gig?" Dan demanded.

"You may need someone to do the heavy lifting," Rob said.

In moments, one of Ames's people dug out a security map of the building. "Our best bet is to go up these fire stairs," Ames said, pointing on the diagram to the near corner of the building. "They shouldn't be affected by that structural crack, and they're as far from the labs as possible." He took a deep breath. "That's where the fire is. We can only hope that nothing else goes up."

"Fine. Let's go." Mr. Swift glanced at the map just long enough to note where Frayne's office was located. Carrying axes and power saws, Tom and Dan followed the older men into the building. Rob brought up the rear.

Running down the main hallway of the

Bomb Palace, the rescuers began to cough and choke. The air inside the building was hot, and the thin wisps of smoke from the fire had a burning, chemical smell to them.

"Air masks," Mr. Swift snapped, not even stopping as he slipped into his protective gear.

Tom could tell his father was upset. The mask covered Mr. Swift's face, but his eyes expressed his fear for Sandra. Tom had never seen his dad climb four flights of stairs so fast.

As Mr. Swift went to open the fire door at the fifth-floor stairwell, Tom took his arm.

"Dad," he said, pointing to a suspicious-looking crack in the wall above the door, "maybe this is a job for Rob."

Mr. Swift nodded, and the rescuers retreated to the landing below as Rob tested the door. "Seems to be a little stuck," the robot's voice came to them. "Whoa!"

With a crash, debris came tumbling down the stairs. Tom and the others flattened themselves against the wall. "Rob!" he called up. "Are you all right?"

For a moment there was silence, and then they heard the sound of shifting rubble. A very dusty Rob came back down the stairs. "Good thing I opened that door instead of you, sir," he said to Mr. Swift, rubbing a brand-new dent in his head. "The ceiling's completely collapsed in this section."

Tom's father immediately headed for the fourth-floor door. "We'll cross this floor to another stairway," he said. "Which ones are the nearest?"

Harlan Ames led the way across the floor, which seemed hardly damaged.

"Do you have any idea what caused the explosion?" Tom asked as they walked.

Ames grunted. "In a building full of explosives, you could probably take your pick," he said. "But apparently there was more than one bomb set. You wouldn't have the top floors damaged plus the fire downstairs otherwise."

"Maybe the fire was set to keep anyone from coming upstairs," Tom said. "Then the whole building could be destroyed."

They reached the new set of stairs and sent Rob up to test the door. "All clear," he reported.

Incredibly, when they stepped through the fire door, that section of the fifth floor seemed completely untouched. However, Tom noticed cracks in the ceiling and a low grinding sound coming from overhead. "We'd better move," he said.

Harlan Ames led them down a pair of corridors, then stopped. "Frayne's office is about halfway down there," he said, pointing.

The far end of the corridor looked as if a giant had tromped hard on the roof and knocked everything down onto the floor.

"Well," Mr. Swift said quietly, "now we know why we couldn't come from the opposite direction."

They started down the hallway, spreading out as if afraid to put too much weight on any one part of the floor. "Five-thirty, five-thirty-two—here it is. Five-thirty-four." Mr. Swift took a deep breath as he opened the door.

The office was right on the edge of the cave-in zone. One wall had disappeared in a pile of rubble, and the ceiling tilted at an alarming angle. A steel I beam slanted across a desk. Under that desk, Tom saw an unmoving human leg.

His stomach flip-flopped as he dropped to one knee, afraid of what he was about to see.

Then he sighed. "It's better than I thought," he said. "She's in a clear pocket under here. But the front of the desk is too low to move her from under it."

"No problem," Dan said, starting up his saw.

"No!" Tom said. "We can't cut through the desk. It's the only thing keeping that beam off Sandra."

Above them, ceiling beams creaked as more debris settled with a deep, rumbling noise.

"We'll have to move the desk—and Sandra—right away." Mr. Swift's voice was tight.

"I'll handle the beam," Rob said, positioning himself.

Tom and Dan took the edges of the desk. Mr. Swift and Harlan Ames leaned underneath, grabbing Sandra's leg and an arm. "All right," Mr. Swift said. "On the count of three. One, two, *now!*"

Rob strained upward against the beam. Dan and Tom shifted the desk while Mr. Swift and Harlan Ames scooted Sandra out from under the beam. Mr. Swift gathered his daughter up in his arms, and they all retreated to the doorway. Tom called, "Drop it, Rob."

The robot let go of the beam and moved back. With a roar, rubble cascaded to the space where Sandra had been just seconds before.

The whole building shook as the older men hustled down the hall, moving Sandra in a fireman's carry. Her head lolled back, and under a coating of plaster dust, her face was deathly pale. She was still breathing, though, and that was the important thing.

They dashed down the fire stairs to the first floor, emerging into deeper smoke. This stairway was closer to the labs than the ones they had used to go up.

"Let's get out of here," Mr. Swift said.

"This way?" Rob asked, pointing down a corridor.

"No. This side hallway is faster." Harlan Ames kicked open a set of swinging doors, only to reveal another corridor, thick with greenish smoke.

"Doesn't look too good," Ames said, "but there's a side exit about twenty yards ahead."

Together, he and Mr. Swift stepped into the reeking cloud, still carrying Sandra. Tom and Dan followed them. Then Tom caught a glimpse of something moving up ahead. "Hey, there's—"

He didn't get a chance to finish.

A heavy metal rod swung out to catch Harlan Ames on the shoulder.

Ames, Mr. Swift, and Sandra fell to the floor.

7

HARLAN AMES LET GO OF SANDRA, GRABBING for his pistol in its holster. Somehow, the unknown attacker could see through the billowing clouds. The attacker could move quickly, too. As the security chief raised his gun, the attacker struck again, knocking the pistol from Harlan's hand.

The rescuers' only weapon flew off into the smoke, landing with a clatter somewhere in the hallway.

That wasn't the only problem. Without an air mask, Sandra was gasping, her body racked with choking coughs. "Help me get her out of here!" Mr. Swift cried.

Tom joined his father, and he and Harlan helped move the semiconscious girl back to the swinging doors. Dan stood guard against the attacker.

He started up the power saw, saying, "Back off, sucker, or I'll slice you in two!"

The saw buzzed ominously as Dan waved it blindly in the smoke, trying to cover his friends' retreat.

Just as they reached the swinging doors, the invisible attacker struck again. The metal rod swooped out of the murk in the hall, obviously with a lot of weight behind it. Dan's chain saw shrieked wildly as the metal smashed into it. Then both rod and saw bounced back from each other.

Dan just managed to avoid slicing himself in two as he was flung back. The saw left his hands, slashing its way through the doorway. Tom managed to grab his friend and haul him to safety as the others dove through the doorway.

The air was a little clearer on the other side of the doors, although now smoke began to billow through the hole Dan's saw had sliced. Harlan reached over to turn off the still-vibrating saw. Mr. Swift placed an extra air mask on Sandra. "Should have done that before," he said, shaking his head. "I'm really losing it tonight."

He glanced at the others, especially Harlan Ames. "I thought you told me the building was empty."

"Guess I was wrong," Ames said. "Looks like maybe we've got the bomb setter stuck in here with us."

"And where's Rob?" Tom suddenly said. "His eyes would be able to cut through the crud in there."

"Sorry, Tom," a voice came from behind them. Rob moved up the hallway, his usually gleaming outer skin now discolored with streaks of chemical smoke as well as concrete dust. "I was checking out the area of the fire, and there's danger—"

An enormous *whooomp!* behind him knocked the robot and everyone else flat on the floor. Something blazing hot flew down the hallway over their heads, smashing the swinging doors to splinters before disappearing into the smoke beyond.

"Well, I don't think we'll be going that way," Tom said, staring at the now-raging fire behind them. "And we've got a nut with a metal rod waiting for us on the other way out. Want to take a look in there and find him, Rob?"

The robot didn't respond.

"Rob?"

"What's his problem?" Dan asked.

Tom knelt over the robot, looking puzzled. "If I didn't know any better, I'd say he was unconscious—and that's something he's not programmed for."

"We've got to get out of here," Mr. Swift said. "And that means getting past our friend with the rod."

"Especially since by now, he may have found my gun," Harlan Ames added under his breath.

Tom abruptly stood up, tossing Dan the ax he'd been carrying. "Here's a weapon for you. Harlan, pick up the chain saw." He looked up and down the hall. "There's one lab here that is still reasonably far enough from the flames. We'll head for it."

"Tom, the labs have no windows—and no exits," his father pointed out.

The rod came swishing out of the greenish cloud, just missing Harlan Ames's head as he ducked. Snatching up the saw, the security chief set the chains to snarling. He and Dan fought the stranger in the murk while Tom and his father helped Sandra into the lab.

They set the girl gently down on the floor. "Now what?" Tom's father asked tiredly.

"We fight back, using the weapons at hand," Tom said. "Come on, Dad. This is an explosives lab. We should be able to find something."

Together, they searched through the chemicals on the shelves. From outside came shouts and the sounds of confused fighting.

"They're not going to last very long," Tom's father said worriedly.

Tom had a jar in one hand and was busily scanning labels. "Any phosphorus or sulfur over there, Dad?"

Mr. Swift passed a couple of jars to his son. "How can that nut with the rod even see anything with the air full of chemicals?"

"Did you notice how strong he was?" Tom said, carrying a bunch of jars to a lab table. "When he swung at Dan's saw, the rod went back, but he didn't fall over like Dan. Come on."

He picked up a beaker, poured some chemicals into it, then took a jar from his father, preparing to add it to his mixture.

"Are you sure you know what you're doing?" Mr. Swift said, watching over Tom's shoulder. "When they mix—"

Outside, another fireball flew past. For a second they saw figures silhouetted against the glass in the door. Harlan Ames shouted wildly as he was knocked to the floor.

"I know what I'm doing, Dad." Tom poured the third ingredient into the beaker. "Now I've got ten seconds. . . ."

Even as he spoke, he ran to the door, yanked it open, and threw the beaker out into the hallway. He just made it—the glass mixing bowl was becoming hot in his hand.

The chemical mixture exploded, blowing

the murk away for a moment. And in that moment, Tom grabbed up a lab bench and charged into the battle.

Harlan Ames was down, the saw knocked halfway down the hallway. Looming over him was a robot, a long metal rod raised in its spindly arms. But this wasn't one of the utility robots usually found in the Bomb Palace. This machine was tall and ungainly, on caterpillar tracks—a maintenance robot from the data center.

Using the bench as a battering ram, Tom smashed the machine in the side, sending it teetering. The machine was still able to whip around, swinging the metal rod like a baseball bat.

But Dan, at last able to see his opponent, went into a counterswing with his ax, catching the rod on the ax head. The impact nearly knocked Dan down. He staggered, but the robot was the one who went crashing to the floor.

Whirring, its motors whining, the robot tried to push itself upright. But Tom, Dan, and Harlan all leapt to the attack, smashing down on the robot with all their strength. The spindly arms went first, bent and battered. Even the body of the robot was dented and bashed as the smoke rolled in again.

"Come on," Tom panted, "it's finished.

Let's grab my father and Sandra and get out of here."

Carefully, they picked up Sandra Swift and headed down the hallway again. Her eyes fluttered open, and she looked dazedly around. "Wha—?" she managed to say.

"There was an accident, honey, but you're all right." Her father's voice was soft as he explained to her. "We're just getting you out now."

"Oh?" Sandra said. "Oh. Good." Her head leaning against her father's shoulder, she passed out again.

Harlan Ames's face was full of worry as he looked from Sandra to Tom. "That was nice work," he said. "What do you think a maintenance robot was doing here? Could it have planted the bombs? And why did it attack us?"

"I suspected you were fighting a robot— what else could see in this smoke? As to why it attacked . . ." Tom just shook his head.

"Hey, what about Rob?" Dan asked as they walked along. "He's still knocked out, or whatever. You can't leave him here."

Tom shrugged. "We can't take him, either. No way can we carry Rob. He's just too heavy. If the fire doesn't spread, maybe we can get a team in to reclaim him."

At that moment, Tom tripped over something—something that rolled along the floor.

He froze in his tracks, staring down at the featureless silvery ball at his feet.

"Orb told me he was at the data center," Tom said quietly. "So how come he and a maintenance robot are right at ground zero for this sabotage?"

8

O<small>RB, LET'S GET THIS STRAIGHT,"</small> TOM SAID.

"All right, Tom," the round robot replied, sitting in the middle of Mr. Swift's desk. "We can go over it again."

"You took over a maintenance robot and reprogrammed it to take you to the Bomb Palace."

"To the Explosive Compounds Laboratory, yes," the calm voice agreed.

"And once you were inside the lab, you had the robot set two bombs," Tom went on.

"Correct again," Orb said calmly. "It was very slow. We were half an hour behind schedule. Then the maintenance robot proved to be too slow to let us escape."

"And when we came along, you knocked

out Rob and had the maintenance robot attack us."

"Yes," Orb said. "But again, the maintenance robot was too slow. I think it must be a defective machine."

"I don't believe this," Dan Coster said, shifting around on the office couch. "He's confessed to everything!"

"So, you admit to all of this," Tom said. "But *why* did you do it?"

"I did as I was ordered," Orb said. "I followed my programming."

"Who gave the orders?" Tom asked. "Who programmed you?"

For once, Orb's reasonable voice didn't respond immediately. The robot sat in silence for a moment. Its reply, when it came, was halting. "I have no memory of being programmed," Orb finally said. "This is very strange."

"But not surprising." Tom's father paced around the office as he'd been doing ever since he'd gotten back from the hospital. Sandra was all right, but the strain of the incident showed on Mr. Swift's face. Now he glared at Orb. "Dan, you look at a robot like Rob, who can talk slang and even show a certain sense of humor, and you probably see a thinking being. He—or rather, *it*—isn't. Rob and Orb are just machines, with the benefit of some brilliant programming by my son."

Mr. Swift frowned. "Now it seems someone else has been programming them, and as a result, my daughter is in the hospital."

He gave a deep sigh. "Thank heavens she wasn't badly hurt. The doctors think she'll be up and around again by late tomorrow. But this whole situation is deeply disturbing."

"Look on the bright side, Mr. Swift," Dan said. "At least you caught your industrial spy."

"We caught only the spy's information pipeline," Harlan Ames said, shaking his head. "And now we understand why no prototypes got handed over. Orb has no hands."

"We're just lucky he wasn't with Rob," Tom said. "If Orb had had more capable help . . ." He stopped, a deep frown on his face. "Those bombs would have gone off half an hour earlier, and your office phones would have been all tied up, taking care of the emergency." He paused for a second. "Right about the time that Rick was kidnapped."

Mr. Swift nodded. "It was all planned as a distraction. Very clever." He began pacing the room again. "The whole operation was clever. First, I learn that there seems to be a leak high in my organization—perhaps in security. That's so I won't talk to you about it, Harlan."

Ames nodded.

"Then come threats of sabotage—no, I

didn't talk to you about them, Tom. I didn't talk to anybody. With a spy among us, anything I said might be recorded. So, I took the quiet way. I tightened security and tried to make sabotage impossible. It didn't work out too well."

He rubbed a hand against his eyes. "Whoever pulled this off knows me better than I know myself. The person pressed all the right buttons. And that's what *really* scares me."

Mr. Swift stopped beside his desk, looking down at Orb. "Well, at least we can start repairing the damage we know about. You'll have to turn Orb off, of course, and get him reprogrammed."

"I expected that." Tom opened a long case that sat on the desk top. Inside was a six-inch-long, magnetically coded needle. He rolled Orb over until he found an almost invisible pinhole in the robot's silvery metal skin. "Sorry about this, Orb," Tom said as he prepared to slide the needle in.

"I understand, Tom," Orb said. "Protecting programming is veruuuurrrrrrrrrrrr." The robot's voice ran down as the needle slid home.

"A copy of Orb's programming is stored in the computer center," Tom said. "After I check it over to make sure nobody's tampered with it, Orb will be as good as new again."

"That's still a scary thing to see," Dan said, a little shudder running down his back.

Mr. Swift handed the deactivated robot to Ames. "That's only part of the problem solved."

"Right," Ames said. "Now comes the time-honored question: Who done it?"

"We'll turn Orb over to the programming department and see if they can find any clues in the way he was programmed. Maybe our spy left some computerized fingerprints," Mr. Swift said.

"You know," Tom said, "the fact that the spy has to be a programmer makes this guy Frayne a more solid suspect."

"You've got a point," Dan said. "Mr. Ames, you say this guy has a new supply of money coming from nobody knows where."

Harlan Ames nodded. "We even got a look into his bank account. The money doesn't seem to come in checks. It comes in cold cash."

Dan nodded. "Frayne is a programmer, which means he could monkey with Orb. And isn't it interesting which building gets blown up? The Bomb Palace—right where he works."

Ames shook his head. "I'd hate to go to the police with a case like that. They'd laugh me right out of headquarters. The evidence is all circumstantial."

"Still," Tom said, "Frayne would be worth

checking on. If he passed the information about the test, for instance, that means he must have a connection nearby. And *that* means maybe we'd have a connection to Rick."

They all sat in silence for a moment, turning that thought over. Then the intercom on Mr. Swift's desk buzzed.

"Excuse me, sir," the guard at the desk outside said. "I've got a call for your son from a Mandy Coster. She says it's important."

Tom immediately picked up the phone. "Mandy, does this mean what I think it means? You found him? Great work! Where are you? Uh-huh. I'll be there right away."

He turned to the others in the room. "Speaking of Garret Frayne, Mandy has just tracked him down—in the Central Lanes bowling alley. I'm on my way there." He handed the deactivated Orb to Dan. "Could you bring him down to programming and have them start checking him out? Thanks." He headed for the door.

Central Lanes was the largest building in a shopping strip that had known better times. That message came through clearly from the bowling alley's neon sign, which flashed in huge letters: CENT AL LANES.

The *R* in the sign hadn't worked since Tom and his family had arrived in town, five years before. But in spite of the sign and the splotchy concrete walls, there were plenty of cars parked outside Central Lanes and lots of kids inside.

After walking through the door, Tom, now wearing a fresh white shirt over clean khaki slacks, had to spend a moment or two looking around the place before he spotted Mandy at the snack bar. She was talking to a guy who obviously couldn't believe that she wanted him to get lost.

Tom moved closer and joined them.

"—been hanging around for I don't know how long and he hasn't shown," the guy was saying. "Why not give up on him? Especially when you've got *me* here."

"Hi, Tom." Mandy gave him a look that Tom usually saw in cowboy movies when the cavalry arrived.

"Sorry I'm late," Tom said, picking up his cue from what the guy had said.

"That's okay. I was just talking with Jerry here. Jerry, meet Tom."

"Great to meet you," Jerry said. "Hey, it's my frame. Catch you later, okay?" He headed back to the lanes.

"Want a soda?" Tom asked.

"I've had three since I came in here," Mandy said. "The counter people think I'm dying of thirst. Jerry and his pals all think I want to make friends, but I wanted to stay someplace where I could keep an eye on Frayne." She nodded across the room. "He's on lane four."

Tom looked over to see Garret Frayne about to send his ball down the lane. His dark hair was longer than in his hologram file picture. He tossed his head to keep his eyes clear before letting the ball go. He rolled a strike.

As Frayne turned back to the other players, he caught sight of Tom and went poker-faced for a moment. Then he put on a big smile and walked over to the snack bar.

"Tom Swift," he said, sticking out his hand. "I'm Garret Frayne—I work for your father." He turned to Mandy. "When I saw this girl standing around, I knew she had to be waiting for somebody special—especially since she turned down my friend Jerry."

Tom didn't shake the hand Frayne held out. "We've met before, Frayne—when somebody sabotaged my skyboard. You were right out on the testing field for that. But I guess you missed the latest piece of sabotage, being in here all night—the big explosion down at Swift Enterprises."

"There was an explosion?" Frayne asked, all innocence.

"Yeah, the Bomb Palace blew up, while my sister was inside. She nearly got killed."

"I didn't—I'm sorry to hear that," Frayne said, shaken.

Tom's voice was quiet, but the tone burned like acid. "I'm so glad to see you have a conscience. It's okay to blow things up, but you don't like to see people get killed. Well, my friend Rick nearly got killed tonight, when your friends kidnapped him. And I was real lucky I didn't end up like a pancake when your pals sabotaged my skyboard test today."

A pair of burning red circles appeared on Frayne's cheeks. "I don't know what you're talking about," he blustered.

"I'm talking about the extra cash you've been spending lately," Tom said, raising his voice. "You know, the money you make as a corporate spy and saboteur?"

"Are you crazy? You're accusing me of something that happened while I was here in front of all these people."

"It was something you set up when you tampered with one of my robots. Just because it happened by remote control doesn't mean you're not responsible." Tom was shouting now. "You earned your dirty money."

"Hey, I don't have to tell you anything about my money," Frayne shouted back. "Maybe I won the lottery. Or maybe my great-uncle Julius left it to me in his will. I don't see where I have to answer to you about any of it."

"Oh, you'll answer sooner or later," Tom told him. "I may not be able to go to the police yet, but I'll be looking for ways to make your life miserable." He grabbed the front of Frayne's shirt. "Understand?"

Frayne pushed his hand away, and Tom threw an awkward punch. Frayne blocked it and knocked Tom to the floor. Tom was up again like a shot, and they grappled wildly for a moment, until Frayne got a leg behind Tom's heel, tripped him, and sent him to the floor again.

By now, the three guys who'd been bowling with Frayne were standing beside him. "Maybe you'd better leave now," Jerry said.

Frayne just waved them away. "Hey, guys, I don't need any help against Tom Wimp," he said. "Unless maybe he decides to send a robot after me."

Tom and Mandy left the bowling alley on a tide of mocking laughter. Walking him to his car, Mandy darted only one quick look to his face. "Tom, I'm sorry—" she started to say.

But Tom began laughing. "Well, if you're so embarrassed for me, I guess Frayne is convinced he beat me fair and square."

He opened the passenger-side door for Mandy, then slipped in behind the wheel, holding out his hand to her. "Do you know what this is?"

She stared at the tiny object in his palm. "A straight pin?" she said.

"A microminiaturized bug," Tom said. "I

planted one on Frayne while we were tussling. Let's hear what he's broadcasting now."

Tom pulled a small box out of the glove compartment—a combined radio receiver and microcassette recorder. He turned it on and began recording.

"—kay guys, excuse me a minute." Frayne's voice came through loud and clear. They heard a moment of crowd noises, the clink of coins, then a snatch of dial tone. "He's at the pay phone," Tom said, turning up the volume. They could clearly hear the touch-tone beeps as Frayne dialed.

"I slipped this onto his collar, so it would be nearby if he called someone," Tom said as they listened to a phone ringing.

"Yes?" a cold voice said.

"It's Frayne."

"You're not supposed to call this number unless you've got very hot information."

"I've got hot info, all right," Frayne said. "Tom Swift came up to me just now and accused me of nearly killing his sister with a bomb. They're onto me, man, and I want the rest of the money you promised me."

Frayne's voice turned ugly. "It looks like your big boss, the Black Dragon, didn't plan this as well as he thought."

9

TOM LEANED FORWARD, CONCENTRATING ALL his attention on the receiver.

"You'll see your money," the cold voice on the phone told Frayne, "after the package heads east in the morning. Don't call us here again. We'll be in touch."

"Listen—" Frayne began, but the only response he got was the click of the phone being hung up.

Mandy stared wide-eyed at the receiver-recorder, as Tom shut it off. "That was outrageous," she said.

"And worth the lumps I took planting the bug on him," Tom said. "You heard the guy on the other end referring to a 'package.' How much would you bet that package's name is Rick Cantwell?"

"But who is this Black Dragon guy?" Mandy said. "The one who's supposed to be the big boss?"

"I've heard the name before," Tom said. "Whenever my father hears it, he changes the subject somehow." He frowned. "Well, I don't think he'll be able to pull that trick this time."

"Um, great," Mandy said, looking at her watch. "I feel really dumb for bringing this up at a time like this, but I just saw what time it is."

Tom glanced at his watch. "It's incredibly late, and you should be heading home," he said.

"If you want to just leave me—" Mandy began.

Tom shook his head. "I'll follow you."

As he drove after Mandy's car, Tom felt like a tire with a slow leak. Things had gone pretty well with Mandy tonight—as long as he was distracted, fighting and planning to help Rick. Now, though, he didn't even know what to say.

Mandy parked in front of her house, then came over to Tom's car and stood by the window. "I guess this is goodbye," she said.

Tom nodded. "I've got to get this tape back to the complex."

She surprised him by leaning in the window and planting a kiss on his cheek. "I'll tell you one thing, Swift," Mandy said. "You sure aren't a dull date."

Tom grinned all the way back to the Swift Enterprises complex.

He was lucky enough to run into Harlan Ames right near the entrance gate, and he gave him the tape for analysis. Then Tom reported to his father.

Mr. Swift couldn't believe their luck in getting a telephone link to the kidnappers. "You say they haven't moved him yet?" he repeated.

"That's what the voice on the other end of the phone told Frayne," Tom said. "Frayne also mentioned the person who's supposed to be in charge of the whole operation—the Black Dragon."

Mr. Swift sank into the chair behind his desk. He sighed, placing his hands flat on the table.

"Come on, Dad, you pull this silence routine whenever that name comes up. Do you know who this guy is?"

"I knew him once," Tom's father said. "His real name is Xavier Mace."

Tom frowned. "Mace. . . . Wait a second. I've read some of his papers in genetics."

"You'd have to if you were going to learn anything about the subject," Mr. Swift said. "Mace's early papers were the foundations for a lot of later breakthroughs."

"They were brilliant," Tom said.

"That's a good description of Xavier Mace. He's a rare scientist—an incredible researcher who also can turn his theories into something practical."

"Sounds like you, Dad."

Tom Swift, Sr., shook his head, then picked up a pen at his desk and fingered it, seemingly distracted by an old memory. "There's one big difference. Mace never lets *anything* stand in the way of his research—not ethics, not the environment, not even human life." He shuddered. "If ten thousand people have to die to prove a scientific point for him, then they die."

"You can't mean that."

"Oh, I can," Mr. Swift said. "About fifteen years ago, Mace was up for a Nobel prize. He'd been researching the genetics of twins, the old nature-or-nurture thing. Is a person's character formed by the genes he's born with or by the way he's brought up?"

Tom frowned, puzzled. "What's so awful about that?"

Mr. Swift tightened his grip on the pen he'd been fiddling with. "He'd based his theories on the so-called research the Nazis did in their death camps, where they butchered countless numbers of twins."

"That's pretty awful," Tom murmured.

"It gets worse. When the Nobel committee discovered this and rejected his work, Mace devoted himself to making money. I think he's also been revenging himself on the world. His companies pollute more water, build more weapons, and destroy more lives than any organization on Earth. He looks on most people as mere laboratory rats in his experiments."

"You're putting that pretty strongly," Tom said.

Mr. Swift opened a drawer in his desk. "I have a file here, compiled over the years. It has evidence that the African drought was caused by a failed Mace experiment in weather control. There's *proof* that he virtually runs several Third World countries. Once he gets control of the government, he builds dangerous nuclear and chemical plants right in the middle of populated areas. He virtually enslaves workers for his manufacturing plants. When he's finished, nothing grows where he's been because of the toxic waste he leaves behind."

"This guy sounds like a real monster," Tom said.

"He's the exact opposite of everything you and I believe in," Mr. Swift told his son as he rose from behind the desk. "I knew that sooner or later we'd have to fight him. Mace looks on Swift Enterprises as his only real rival in theoretical science. He's been preparing to destroy us for five years—ever since he bought up our old complex back in Lake Carlopa."

"He bought our plant back in New York?" Tom exclaimed. "If you know so much about him, how did you let him do that?"

"Xavier Mace doesn't operate out in the open," Mr. Swift explained, walking to the window and staring at the remains of the Bomb Palace. "He deals through agents who work for companies, who report to people who obey him—like the spy who worked under our noses. We sold the plants to what seemed like a reputable company—which turned out to be a front for the Black Dragon."

Tom's father shook his head bitterly. "He turned the place into a fortress—his headquarters. In the process, he's just about ruined the town."

"So now he wants the secret of my superconductor," Tom said. "And he's going to leave a Mace-size hole in anyone who gets in his way. Is that it?"

"He certainly has one of your skyboards, and maybe the other one. When our people went to clean up the site by the beach, they found no trace of your board—and a large piece cut out of your track there. And he has Rick to ask for technical details." Mr. Swift turned from the window and saw his son pacing in an agitated fashion from one end of the room to the other.

"But Rick doesn't know any technical

details—and in the hands of a guy like the Black Dragon, that's probably a very dangerous situation." Now Tom stopped to rub the back of his neck. "We have to get Rick back—and fast."

Harlan Ames burst through the door. "We've got them now," he announced, waving a computer printout. "That number Tom came back with is supposed to be out of service. It's assigned to a line shack for an old ranch that supposedly went belly-up years ago. And guess where it is? Right in the middle of the area where that chopper disappeared from radar."

"A telephone number that never got reassigned, and calls still go through to it," Tom said. "Sounds like someone has been having fun with the phone company's computer."

"Well, it's our turn for fun," Ames said. "The local police are going in there now, and our security people are giving them assistance." He looked at Tom. "Want to come along in my chopper?"

"You got it!" Tom said. "Let's stop by my lab—I have some equipment that might help on this raid."

As soon as they were airborne, Tom gave an infrared visor to Ames. "I can't get over this thing," the security man said, staring out the nose of the helicopter. "I can see the ground clearly, and this doesn't flatten things out, like regular IR gear does."

He shook his head as they flew on. "Too bad you didn't have more to give to the raiding party."

Using his own visor, Tom easily made out the road that led to their destination. The heat exhaust of the raiding force's vehicles lit it up brightly in infrared.

"Kind of surprising, don't you think, that these guys would hole up in a box canyon?" Tom asked Ames. "I mean, a hideout with only one exit doesn't sound like a good idea."

Ames shrugged. "One way out also means only one way in to defend. Then, too, this is a pretty isolated area. They wouldn't have to worry about people stumbling over them."

He pulled the helicopter back over the caravan of off-road vehicles making their way up the rugged trail. "And there is another way out of that canyon. They've got a helicopter. Of course," Ames said, grinning and patting the control panel of his machine, "we've got one up here that's ready to sit on them."

At last, the police and security vehicles had reached the long, thin neck of valley that connected the canyon with the rest of the world. They must also have passed a guard, because the small base camp in the canyon came on the alert.

Lights went on, and Tom could make out

the figures of men running desperately out of camouflaged tents around the canyon wall. Headlights shone from the noses of several trucks that took off into the valley. Soon enough, they'd encounter the police.

"We've got them bottled up," Ames said happily, bringing his chopper to cover the airspace above the canyon. "Let's go and push the cork down from the top."

He circled over the canyon, unclipping his microphone as he went. He spoke into the mike, and loudspeakers under the helicopter amplified his voice. "YOU ARE SURROUNDED," Ames said. "COMPLETELY TRAPPED. THERE IS NO WAY OUT. SURRENDER NOW."

They started a second circuit of the canyon, with Ames giving the same disheartening message. "YOU ARE SURROUNDED. COMPLETELY TRAPPED. WHAT THE—"

A huge section of camouflage netting fell away in the center of the canyon, revealing a VTOL Harrier jet—a vertical takeoff and landing plane.

The jet fighter had obviously been prepared for flight. As soon as the netting was out of the way, the Harrier roared straight up, flames streaming from its engines.

It went by Harlan Ames's chopper the way a motorcycle passes a turtle. Turbulence from the jet exhaust shook the helicopter as if it were a toy.

The microphone flew from Harlan's hand, but Tom caught the mike and hung it back on its hook.

"What do you say we head back to the complex?" he said bitterly. "We both know that the person we came for just left on that jet."

10

INSIDE THE HARRIER, RICK CANTWELL SAT back in his flight seat. He didn't have much choice about that. In addition to the belt and safety harness that restrained him, two sets of handcuffs bound each wrist to a chair arm.

He turned to the man sitting beside him, one of the thinnest guys Rick had ever seen. But it was a hard, lean thinness that spoke of stringy muscles. This guy was probably a lot stronger than he looked. The stranger had shoulder-length hair, pure white. There was a hint of pale eyes beneath the sunglasses he wore, and his pasty white, unlined face showed no emotion at all. Talk about your bad-looking dudes! Rick thought. The guy even dressed the part. He wore a black shirt with rolled-up sleeves, black jeans, and cowboy boots.

"Mind telling me what's going on?" Rick said. "I get snagged in midair, and somebody puts me in a plastic-foam cocoon with an oxygen mask on my face—for how long, I don't know. Then all of a sudden, you cut me out of there, hustle me into this plane, and we take off. I suppose I should thank you for getting me out of that plastic, but"—Rick rattled his handcuffs—"somehow I don't think you were there to rescue me."

The man in black barely turned his head toward Rick. "You talk too much" was all he said.

"I just want to know why you marched me around in the dark—"

The man's mouth changed its line for a second in the barest of smiles. "You were about to be rescued. We couldn't have that, Cantwell."

"How do you know—stupid question," Rick said. "I had my wallet in my pocket when you got me, and I don't feel myself sitting on it now." Rick sat back in his seat. So he'd almost been rescued! He had to keep his spirits up. "You know, I had at least eight bucks in that wallet. I hope you'll—"

"If you're going to talk, you'd better talk about something useful, like those boards." The stranger pointed, and Rick saw that the two boards from the test were stowed beside him. Apparently, Tom's had cracked on impact, but Rick's was intact.

"The inside of the broken one glowed for a while," the stranger said. "Is that what makes this superconductor work at room temperature? Something inside the board itself?"

"Why should I tell you?" Rick said. This guy looked as if he had no problems with killing people. If Rick wanted to stay alive long enough to be rescued again, he'd have to convince the guy he was useful. Maybe pretending to know about Tom's superconductor would do the trick. "Unless, of course, you want to make a deal."

The man grabbed Rick by the neck, turning Rick's head so he could look into his eyes. "You don't seem to understand things yet." Hard fingers dug painfully into Rick's skin. "You're in no position to bargain. You'll just tell us what we want to know."

The man's quiet confidence was more frightening than any threats could have been. He let go of Rick and pulled a small Swiss army knife from his pocket. "These things can be real useful if the little gadgets on it are used creatively." He swung out the corkscrew attachment. "Just think for a minute how this could work . . . if I decided to use it on your face."

The point of the corkscrew was inches from

Rick's left eye when a screen on the panel in front of the stranger lit up. He quickly whipped the knife away as a face formed on the screen. It was a gentle face, almost fatherly, with a shock of salt-and-pepper hair and chubby cheeks. "I'm not pleased, Cougar."

"The Swift people discovered our base camp somehow," answered the man in black. "I put the boards, the track sample, and the prisoner on board the plane and got out of there."

"Just one jump ahead of the police." The eyes of the image turned deadly cold. "That's not the way I—or my operatives—are supposed to work, Cougar."

"Yes, sir."

"And, Cougar—don't touch the prisoner. I'll expect you here in three hours."

For the rest of the flight, the man called Cougar didn't speak to Rick. He didn't even glance at him, or so Rick thought until he caught a reflection in the glass canopy. Cougar wasn't just looking at him from behind. He was glaring at Rick in hatred.

When the plane landed, it was met by a black limo with the word *UNITECH* stenciled on the door. Rick sat in the luxurious vehicle, his hands cuffed behind him and Cougar at his side. Staring out the tinted window, Rick studied everything he could see. He might get a clue to where he was—or how he could escape.

He knew the plane had flown east. And from the look of the country—rolling farmlands with distant mountains—he seemed to be somewhere in the Northeast, anyplace between upstate New York and Maine.

They passed through a small industrial town, and then the limo stopped at a barrier in the road. Rick saw a large lake off to the left. The driver slipped a data-key into a slot in a concrete slab, and the barrier slid away.

"Abandon all hope, kid." Cougar spoke up for the first time in hours. "You've just entered the Dragon's lair."

"What are you talking about?" Rick said.

Cougar studied his young captive for a moment. "You have no idea you've been taken by the Black Dragon, do you?" He shook his head. "In this case, what you don't know can—and probably *will*— hurt you."

The screen shutting them off from the driver suddenly dropped, and the chauffeur handed back two red badges. Rick got a brief view of what was ahead—a large industrial plant—before the screen snapped back up.

Cougar attached one of the badges to Rick's shirt pocket. Then he pinned the other glowing red dot to his own shirt.

"What's this?" Rick asked.

"It might keep you from getting zapped." Cougar gave Rick another one of his thin smiles. "You'll see."

The car passed through another checkpoint, this time in a tall metal wall, then stopped. Cougar opened the door and pulled Rick out. Rick stood in the sunlight, blinking at the scene before his eyes.

Everywhere he looked there were long, flat, squared-off buildings laid out in neat rows with interconnecting streets. The design of the place reminded him of the Swift complex back home. But these once-shiny and modern buildings were grimy, their paint peeling, as if no one had bothered with them for years. And something had been added—bridges, platforms, and sloping ramps that connected with the higher stories of the buildings. It wasn't just that the additions were ugly; they looked like cancers that had grown on a healthy, beautiful body. They turned what had been a well-proportioned layout into a fantastic yet dismal-looking anthill.

Lots of ants *were* rushing around, or in this case, robots. They all came in an identical basic design about five feet tall: Their bases looked like miniature tank treads, their bodies were round, and in place of a humanoid head was a bulb with sensor modules. Many had special tool arms added for various kinds of work. They pulled small trucks of parts or drove larger trucks through the teeming masses. They rushed from building to building, set on completion of their errands.

"Come on," Cougar said, pulling Rick into the street—right into the path of the onrushing horde. Amazingly, the robots whizzed around them. Rick realized that the red badge must have something to do with the machines avoiding them. He glanced back at the limo, to see the driver heading off with the two skyboards under his arms.

"Forget about them," Cougar said. "I'm taking you to your new home."

The small building where he led Rick was separated from the others, although the never-ending flow of robots rushed around it as they did around everything else. Rick had never seen anything to match it, not even at Swift Enterprises. That was a chilling thought.

They arrived at the back door of the building. Cougar slipped on a rubber glove and slid a data-key into a slot. The door opened, and Cougar pushed Rick inside.

He found himself in an empty room with no furniture. On one wall was a larger-size version of the viewscreen he'd seen on the plane.

Cougar pressed a call button on the side of the screen. "He's here," he reported.

The screen came to life immediately, showing the same gentle face Rick had seen before. Seeing it larger, however, Rick caught just a trace of transparency in the image. He wondered if Cougar realized he was taking orders from a hologram.

"Well, you seem to have arrived none the worse for wear," the face said in a kindly voice. "Cougar, remove those handcuffs. Then you can leave."

Shrugging, Cougar undid the cuffs. At the same time, he snatched away Rick's badge. "To keep you from playing in traffic," he said, pocketing the glowing red disk. His gloved hand slipped the data-key into a slot alongside the doorway, and then he stepped out of the room. Rick noticed an electrical crackle in the air as the door slid closed again.

"We'll try to make you as comfortable as possible," the face assured Rick. "You should be our guest for only a few days, while you explain some of the technical details of these superconducting boards."

"Your prisoner, you mean," Rick said, rubbing the angry red marks where the cuffs had bitten into his wrists. He looked around the room, realizing that neither of the two windows had bars.

"I wouldn't think of it," the face in the screen told him. "A high-energy field surrounds the whole building. If you even touch a window, you'll provide a pathway for about half a million volts."

"Thanks for your concern," Rick said.

"Now, as to our business—"

"I only do business with real people, Mr. Black Dragon." Rick forced a confidence into his voice that he didn't feel. "You're just a computerized image."

The hologram was good. Its eyebrows rose, and it looked quite surprised. "Very good, Mr. Cantwell. You have eyes in your head."

"I've got brains in there, too," Rick told him. "If you want my information, I'll make a deal with you. But we have to talk face-to-face."

The projected face smiled and nodded. "I'm about to start analyzing the boards. When I'm finished, we'll talk again."

"Not to a hologram," Rick objected.

"Even to a hologram that packs a punch?" the Black Dragon asked. The image menacingly brought up a hand, then Rick felt as if he'd been hit by a truck.

He was hurtled across the room and slammed against the wall. Then came blackness.

A VERY TIRED TOM SWIFT RUBBED THE PALMS of his hands over his bleary eyes. They felt as if all the sand in the Sahara had blown into them over the course of the sleepless night he'd spent at work. Yawning, he looked up at his early-morning visitor.

"I'm tired because I got up at the crack of dawn to see you," Dan Coster said. "But the way you look—aren't you going to get *any* rest, Tom-Tom?"

Tom told Dan about Frayne's phone call and how the first attempt to rescue Rick had failed. "I'll catch some z's during the flight east," Tom said. "Rob can fly the plane—the guys in the computer center are programming the necessary skills into him right now."

Dan grinned. "A *crash* course, huh?"

That got a ghost of a smile from Tom. "I wouldn't put it *that* way," he said.

"Are you sure Rob can handle the gig, I mean, after Orb knocked him out?"

"Orb just ordered him to turn himself off. You saw how he got up and left with us after I found Orb at the Bomb Palace and figured out what had happened." Tom stifled another yawn, then reached into his pocket for what looked like a pack of mint candy. "That's part of what I did all night—check Rob out."

"What's this buzz I hear about you taking the Rover jet?" Dan asked, holding his hand out for a piece of the candy.

Tom nodded, popping a candy into his mouth. "No, Dan, this isn't a mint, it's something Sandra came up with to help wake me up. It's designed for my specific biochemistry—kind of like a portable cup of coffee, without the negative side effects of caffeine."

Dan smiled. "That's okay. I still like mine in a cup. But what about the Rover?"

"Dad ordered it out of mothballs to help find Rick. But with the building explosion and everything else—well, it wasn't ready for the raid on the Black Dragon's base."

His hands clenched into fists on the lab table. "If we'd been in the Rover, we might have been able to stay on that Harrier's tail, maybe even have forced it down."

Dan put a hand on Tom's shoulder. "I know you're blaming yourself for the spot Rick is in," he said. "But you did your best to save him, just like you'll do your best to save him now." He looked at the complex mass of circuitry Tom was working on. "What are you doing?"

"Pulling together a few surprises for our friend the Black Dragon," Tom said. "If I'm going to play on his home court, I'll need every advantage I can come up with."

The lab door slid open to reveal Tom's father, carrying a duffel bag. "Your mother packed this for you," he said. "Clean socks and things. She knows you're busy, but—"

Tom stepped over to a control panel and punched some keys. "Mom?" he asked.

A holographic image of Mary Swift appeared in the center of the lab. "I was going to call you before you left, but this is better."

The middle-aged and still-beautiful blond woman took a step toward him. "This is more than just goodbye and good luck, Tom. I wanted to talk to you about Xavier Mace."

She took a deep breath and pushed a lock of hair behind an ear. "You see, I knew him. Believe it or not, I actually dated him years ago, before your father and I got together.

He's a brilliant, dangerous man. Remember that," his mother said.

Tom's eyebrows rose. "It's hard to forget, Mom—especially when he's kidnapped my best friend."

"I spent the night thinking about Xavier, trying to come up with some advice for you," Mrs. Swift went on. "This is the best I can say. He was always in love with the sound of his own voice. If you can keep him talking, you might slow him down a little."

Tom looked from his mother to his father, wondering what other adventures they'd been on that he'd never heard about.

His mother gave him a lopsided smile. "I had your father bring you some breakfast, too."

"Right," said Mr. Swift, holding out the other package he was carrying.

"Thanks, Dad—and thanks, Mom."

Still smiling, Mrs. Swift faded away.

Tom took the package from his father and pulled out a bacon-and-egg sandwich. As he ate it his father briefed him for his upcoming flight. "The government has been quite interested in Xavier Mace, even if they can't prove anything against him. They have an agent in Lake Carlopa, who also happens to be an old friend of mine. Phil Radnor has spent the last five years keeping watch on the Lake Carlopa complex—and what the Black Dragon is doing with it," Mr. Swift said. "If anyone can help you get in there and out again with Rick, it's Phil. He's arranged your flight plan and will meet you on the ground."

Tom nodded. "And the Rover? How is it testing out?"

"It checks out fine as a jet and converts perfectly to its Rover form," Mr. Swift said. "It goes from aircraft to ground vehicle in under ninety seconds. We've beefed up the sensors and defenses, too." Tom's father looked grim. "I added a couple of enhanced lasers to give you a little offensive punch. They're linked right into the battle computer. We've been working all night. It should be ready in about half an hour."

"That's just about when I'll be set," Tom said, taking his father's arm. "Thanks, Dad. I know you've gone all out."

"The question is," Tom Swift, Sr., said somberly, "will it be enough?"

When Rick Cantwell came to, he found himself lying in the dark on a cold, concrete floor. He pushed himself up, head aching and arms shaky. Some "punch." The Black Dragon had given him a massive jolt of electricity, enough to throw him against the wall and knock him out.

Walking around to work out the kinks in his muscles, Rick stopped by a window. Evening had fallen, but the ceaseless rush of the robots continued. Rick also noticed that none of the buildings he could see had lights on. Then he realized the robots probably didn't need any light. I'm dealing with an energy-efficient Dragon, he thought.

Also a pretty ruthless one, he realized. How long could he string this guy along with the little information he had? He'd have to do his best until Tom showed up to rescue him.

The thought of Tom started Rick thinking about how his friend would act in a mess like this. First, he'd check out the prison to see what he could use to get out, Rick thought.

That was easy enough. There was nothing in the room he could use—unless he could pry a wall free with his bare hands. The view-screen was immovably set in the wall. And even in the dark, he could see there was nothing else in the room.

He worked his way around the walls, tapping for hollow or weak spots. None. Then Rick tried the floor. It, too, was depressingly solid. Rick found a rough spot in one corner and waited until a truck's moving headlights threw a glimmer through the windows.

It turned out to be a message scratched into the once-wet cement in childish printing. "Tom Swift was here," Rick read, amazed at the coincidence. Under the words was a date from twelve years before. Too bad you're not here now, Rick thought. No, he didn't mean that. Rick wouldn't want his worst enemy in this kind of jam, much less his best friend.

The door opened behind Rick. "You won't last very long if you're staring at the walls already." Cougar's voice had the assurance of a man who'd seen many prison walls. "Get up, kid. The big boss wants to see you."

Rick walked to the open door and stood quietly while Cougar pinned one of the glowing red badges to his shirt. The electron field had been deactivated. For a second, Rick considered jumping Cougar and running for it.

The man's pale eyes bored straight into Rick's. "Don't even think about it, kid. If you try a move on me, I'll have to fix you. And since I have to bring you to the Black Dragon, you'll still have to be mobile. That means I'll have to break your arm."

Cougar gave him another fractional smile. "And when we come back, I'll have to break a leg, so you'll forget about running."

Rick meekly followed his captor out the door.

Out in the dark streets, the high-gear traffic continued as the robot workers rushed blindly along. But though they came close, the machines always veered away from the red badges.

Cougar led the way to a lab building that had not been overbuilt to accommodate the robotic work force. Rick noticed that dim light came out of the windows, as well.

The black-clad guard slipped a data-key into a slot in the door frame, then gestured Rick inside when the door slid open.

This room was much larger than Rick's prison. Track lighting on the ceiling threw a spotlight on a strange little spectacle on the floor. Rick stared at hundreds of toy soldiers—a virtual army, complete with jeeps and tanks.

Then he realized the army was set up on a small oval, in two colors. Part of the oval consisted of strips and pieces of a putty brown substance held together with some sort of insulating tape.

"No doubt you recognize what went into making this experimental setup." Rick turned toward the voice, to find the Black Dragon stepping from the shadows. "We've used pieces of the sample we took from the track where you and Tom Swift ran your ill-fated test."

The Black Dragon shook his head in admiration. "How in the world did you manage to electrify the ceramic itself? The charge drained off when we removed the piece for testing, but my analysis has raised many fascinating questions." He looked toward Rick with raised eyebrows, waiting for him to say something.

"I'd have some questions myself, about a guy who plays with toy soldiers."

Cougar took a step forward from his post by the door, but the Black Dragon waved him back. "I called you here for two reasons. One, so you could speak to me face-to-face, as you asked. The other reason was this experiment—a sort of scale-model test, you might say."

The scientist reached into the pocket of his dark clothing and held out a handful of silvery globes, each about the size of a marble. "Inside these are pieces of the broken skyboard—quite fascinating."

Rick heard the hum of a generator nearby. Then the Black Dragon tossed the spheres over the small-scale track. They floated a couple of inches over the superconductor's surface, like tiny versions of the skyboard.

"Tom Swift used this remarkable material to build a toy—I'll show how it could be a tool." The Black Dragon produced a simple joystick controller and moved the flying marbles into the ranks of toy soldiers. The spheres mowed down rows of plastic fighting men, knocking them over.

"Imagine how much generals would pay for robot troops that could fly into the enemy's ranks, carrying machine guns—or perhaps nerve gas." The plastic army was now completely knocked over. "Or even better . . ."

He moved the flying marbles so they hovered over one of the toy tanks, and then he pressed a button on the top of the joystick. The marbles exploded, leaving the tank a twisted ruin. "Filled with explosives, they'd be the perfect weapon on the battlefield."

"Or for terrorists," Rick said, staring. "As long as you could get your target to stand on top of a giant electromagnet."

"My research department is already overcoming that difficulty," the Black Dragon said. "Sooner or later we'll work our way back from the finished product to the way it was produced. But you could hasten the process of reverse engineering."

The scientist's voice became more demanding. "How are the chargeable crystals made that Swift embedded in Chu's ceramic?"

Rick could see that the moment had come. "It's, uh, one of those deals where an atom is wrapped in a molecule," he said, desperately trying to remember how Tom had described the crystals. "Trapped in a ladder—"

"You mean 'lattice,' I believe." The Black Dragon sounded disappointed. "I also believe you don't have the technical knowledge I need. How unfortunate. I may have to wait until my other spy at Swift Enterprises—the one they haven't detected—discovers the process. It's also most unfortunate for you—you have no usefulness to me."

Cougar stepped forward eagerly, but the Black Dragon halted him by raising a hand. "Of course, you should stay in one piece as a hostage if Tom Swift attempts some move against me. Take him back to his cell, Cougar."

Disappointed, the black-clad man moved to take Rick's arm.

"But," the scientist suggested, "you needn't worry about being *too* gentle."

12

"T OM." ROB'S VOICE SEEMED TO RING IN TOM Swift's ear.

Unwillingly, Tom opened his eyes, to be confronted with the control panel of the Rover. He turned to the copilot's seat, where Rob held the controls. The seat had been specially altered to fit the robot's huge frame, but the sight of the supersonic jet's joystick nearly lost in those enormous hands was still comical.

"We've just passed Scranton, Pennsylvania," Rob said. "It's time to slow down for our descent. I thought you'd want to make the landing on manual control."

"Okay," Tom said, "I'm taking over." Pulling back on the throttle, he brought their air speed down to a mere 500 mph. He didn't want to overshoot their destination—the military reservation near the Green Mountains of Vermont.

A glance out the cockpit showed fog covering the ground below, but the computer screen in the center of the control panel gave him a detailed three-dimensional picture of the terrain they were streaking over. As he started lining up for his approach, Tom stifled a yawn. He'd turned command over to Rob as soon as they were airborne, then dropped off to sleep. But his rest had been barely a catnap. At Mach 2, the trip from coast to coast had taken about two hours.

In moments they were flashing across Lake Champlain, then heading straight for the reservation's classified runway. The landing was smooth, and they taxied toward a high-security hangar.

Standing by the hangar entrance was a big, powerfully built man with a ruddy complexion and graying crew cut—Phil Radnor. As the plane came up, he opened the hangar door and guided them in. Tom cut the engines, and Radnor closed the door.

"We're completely secure in here," he called up as Tom cracked the canopy. "No windows, no bugs, nobody sticking a nose in. This is the best place to convert to the Rover form."

"You heard the man, Rob," Tom said. "Prepare for conversion." They ran down a quick checklist, then Tom keyed in the conversion code on the computer board. The program began to run, and the shape of the plane began to change.

In its jet form, the Rover was a sleek but stubby V shape, with two large engines and delta wings. Now the sharp supersonic nose began to sag as superstructure rods were retracted into the vehicle's body and the carbon-fiber skin was pulled into a bay under the belly. The wings came apart like a Chinese puzzle, swinging over and under the engines and canopy like a clamshell. This gave the vehicle more than automotive styling. The material of the protective wings was laminated ceramic steel, which could resist a five-minute blast from a laser.

The landing gear retracted into the body, while two sets of treads swung out from the vehicle's belly. When the transformation was complete, the Rover seemed to have shrunken in on itself. It had also turned into a vehicle as heavily defended as a tank—but much faster and more maneuverable, powered by a pair of jet-turbine engines.

Phil Radnor shook his head. "I've seen films of that conversion, but it's really something to see in the flesh. We've got clearance to leave it here, as well as permission to store our plane in this sealed hangar. As far as the authorities here are concerned, we off-loaded the Rover from the plane we landed."

"Won't they become suspicious if they look inside and don't find a plane?" Rob asked.

Phil Radnor looked at the robot. "That's why the hangar will be sealed."

Tom punched in the code that would open the clamshell armor and let Radnor in through the vehicle's access hatch. He stood up and shook the older man's hand. "Glad to meet you, Phil. As the resident expert on the Black Dragon, I figured you knew what you were doing when you filed our flight path. But would you mind telling me why you had us land two hours' drive away from Lake Carlopa?"

"Xavier Mace takes a deep interest in all commercial air traffic that passes over or lands near his headquarters," Phil explained. "He monitors it, sweeps it with sensors, and maintains an army of spies in all the local airfields. The military reservation has a lot of top secret comings and goings. And, I hope, it's far enough from the Black Dragon's back-yard that he won't have a lot of informants here."

Tom nodded. "That makes sense."

"I'm sorry to tell you, but the trip to Lake Carlopa is going to take a lot longer than two hours." Phil pulled out a computer disk from his pocket. "I programmed this course for your on-board computer. It avoids all major roads and takes us along routes with maximum protection from air surveillance—and minimum chance of anyone on the ground seeing us. We'll use old logging roads, abandoned trails, and in a couple of places, streambeds. Maybe you think I'm being paranoid, but I've been up against the Black Dragon for five years, and I'm still alive to talk about it."

"You're calling the shots," Tom said. "We'll play it your way."

As they rode along the twisty route, Phil Radnor told Tom something about the changes that had happened to the Lake Carlopa complex. "Mace has turned it into an absolute fortress," he said. "There are electrical booby traps, batteries of lasers, and armed human guards."

Tom shook his head. "It sure doesn't sound like the place I grew up in."

"It's not," Phil agreed. "I just hope you won't be too shocked when you see it."

Phil made them stop at the edge of the woods nearest to what he called his retirement cottage, on the opposite side of a mountain that overlooked the Black Dragon's lair. "As far as anybody knows, I retired as plant manager after UNITECH took the place over," he said. "That's been my cover, but

Mace sometimes has people keeping an eye on me."

He walked across a small clearing in front of the modest cabin and went inside to check his security system. Then he came out, gave the "all clear," and opened the garage door.

The garage was the most interesting part of the property: It was actually built into part of the steep hillside. And as the Rover rolled into the garage, the back wall swung up to reveal a cavernous tunnel.

"This area was built to house a helicopter, if necessary," Phil Radnor explained after Tom and Rob got out of the Rover. "So there's no problem with storing the Rover here. From this point on, though, we'll have to walk."

They headed along the tunnel, which began to slant upward more and more steeply. It started zigzagging in switchbacks and finally turned into a flight of stairs.

Tom was panting by the time they reached the top. "Well, I can see how you keep so fit," he told Phil. "But don't you think an elevator would be easier?"

"No way!" Phil burst out. "Not on this side of the mountain." Then he looked at Tom for a long moment. "You must have headed out of California in a big hurry," he said. "No one told you what the story was here."

"What story?" Tom said.

"Bear with me for one more minute," Phil Radnor said. "Seeing is believing."

They followed a short tunnel, which opened out into the government's advance spying post watchdogging the Black Dragon.

Phil Radnor opened a wooden door, struck a match, and lit a kerosene lantern.

"What—!" Tom exclaimed as he looked around. He'd expected control boards, sensitive scanners, the cutting edge of surveillance technology. Instead he found cameras and an enormous optical telescope.

"Xavier Mace is a very careful man," Phil explained. "His base bristles with sensors guarding against any possible electronic surveillance. We had to come up with an end run, and this was it—*low* tech. There's absolutely nothing electrical up here for his scanners to find. As a matter of fact, I'd feel better if your robot went a little deeper into the mountain right now."

Tom gave the order and Rob retreated, grumbling, back down the tunnel. "Now I see why you don't have an elevator," Tom said. "The electric motor would be a dead giveaway."

"The only electric gear is back by the house," Phil said. "And that has the whole mountain between it and Mace's sensors."

Tom stared around the low-tech wonderland, shaking his head. "You know, this is the kind of stuff my grandfather might have used," he said.

"Do you want a look at the complex?" Phil asked. He went over to the telescope, adjusted the focus, then stepped away from the eye-piece so Tom could see.

Tom peered into the scope and found himself looking down the forested slope of the mountain right into the old Swift complex. Branches had been strategically cut away to give a complete view.

Tom's breath caught in his throat. His memories of the cheerful, shiny-bright plant and of the whole Lake Carlopa area were about as close to paradise as he could imagine. Now, looking through the telescope, it was like seeing an old childhood friend with some horrible, disfiguring disease.

An oily black cloud seemed to hang over the filthy buildings, and virtually identical robots were tearing around almost aimlessly through the streets.

"You told me the place was fully auto-mated except for the guards," Tom said. "I guess I expected to see robots marching in neat rows—not this ant farm approach."

He shuddered and rubbed the back of his tired, aching neck. "Whoever came up with that has a sick mind."

"The question is, what are you going to do about it?" Phil Radnor asked.

Tom Swift squared his shoulders. "I'm going to watch through the telescope while you brief me with everything you know about the guards and defenses down there." He yawned. "Then I'm going to get some sleep while you keep an eye out for any chances of finding Rick."

Tom turned to face Radnor. "Because tonight, sometime after dark, we're going in there."

13

"NICE CATCH, PHIL, SPOTTING THE ROBOT bringing food to that old lab building." Tom pinned a photo of the small structure to the wall. "They must be holding Rick in there— so that's our main target." His finger stabbed at the map of the Black Dragon's complex, pinpointing the location.

"We don't have time to waste on fancy plans. Following the most direct route, we'll go in, grab Rick, and get out as fast as we can. Unless anyone comes up with a good objection, we'll start after one final preparation."

Tom turned a valve on the spraying machine, filling the garage with a greenish fog. It settled on Rob, Phil Radnor, Tom, and everything else in their advance base. Tom didn't worry about ruining anything in the place. It was only an abandoned gas station about a mile from UNITECH's main gate. Tom remembered it as a busy, friendly place from his childhood days. Now the garage was a ruin.

"What is this stuff supposed to do?" Phil Radnor's voice crackled in Tom's earphones. Like Tom, he was dressed as an astronaut, in a black Kevlar and Nomex suit, complete with helmet. Tom had even fitted the helmets with sealed infrared visors. The outfits were bulletproof, fireproof, and gasproof. Standing beside Rob in the green cloud, Tom looked like something out of a science-fiction film.

"I'm spraying us with nonconducting plastic," Tom explained as he ran the fog over them. "I developed it as insulation for my superconductor—but it will also insulate us from any of the Black Dragon's electrical booby traps."

Phil took the sprayer and hosed Tom down. As they headed back to the Rover, they looked no different—except that Rob's usually shiny body was now dulled.

They took their places inside the vehicle. Phil sat behind the wheel, Rob was positioned to operate the sensors, and Tom was at the battle board. Then they headed down the road for the Dragon's lair.

"You know this won't be a surprise attack,"

Phil said. "The Black Dragon has to be expecting you to attempt a rescue. He'll be watching for you."

"He is already," Tom agreed, pointing at the computer-imaged screen. A bird was circling around the car, pacing them. "Crows don't usually fly at night. Let's try something."

He pressed a button on the battle board. The crow swung gracefully around them again, then crashed into a tree.

"The bird was a disguised camera," Tom said. "I jammed its radio controls."

They turned a bend in the road, riding without lights, but the computer image showed them the complex less than a mile away.

"First checkpoint," Phil said, slowing the car.

They pulled up beside an upright cement slab with a slot in it. On either side of the slab a chain-link fence topped with barbed wire marked the boundary with the outside world. A closed gate blocked the roadway.

"Identification," came a mechanical voice from within the slab.

"Sure." Tom reached into his duffel bag and pulled out a white disk about the size of a silver dollar. Cracking the Rover's access hatch slightly, he tossed the disk into the concrete slot. Blue sparks and white smoke belched from the slot, the gate opened, and they were in.

About fifty yards ahead was another checkpoint. "This one has live guards," Phil warned. "They may be upset to see a tank rolling up."

Out of Tom's bag of tricks came a device about the size of a peanut. He twisted the top half one way, the bottom the other, and tossed it out of the hatch. The device sent off a high-pitched whine that they could barely hear through the special filters in their helmets.

The guards could certainly hear it, though. They clapped their hands over their ears. Even so, the vibrations attacked their ears and their brains. In moments, the men dropped to the ground, temporarily paralyzed.

"Two down," Rob said. He stepped from the Rover into the guard shack and pulled the control lever. The heavy gates swung open as he leapt back into the vehicle.

"We're in the laser free-fire zone now," Phil said, hitting the accelerator. The metal wall surrounding UNITECH stood a hundred yards ahead. Every fifty yards, a mast rose above the wall, with what seemed to be a surveillance camera on top. Phil had already told Tom that the squat rectangular boxes were actually laser cannons.

The two lasers closest to the Rover swiveled and fired a burst of light. The inside of the minitank grew noticeably warmer, but the laminate armor held.

"Got to get to the wall before they tag us again," Phil said, punching more power to the treads.

"Sensors show a power surge building under us," Rob suddenly warned.

Phil tried to swerve aside, but the blast of the electronic mine still caught the Rover.

The vehicle was jarred into the air and landed at a sharp angle, throwing Tom against his seat harness. Rob, who wasn't strapped in, hit the wall with enough force to kill a human.

"Another dent." Tom could have sworn the robot sighed.

Phil juiced the treads. They could hear them turning, but the Rover didn't move. "We've got trouble," Phil said.

Another blast of coherent light from the lasers heated up the vehicle.

"Rob," Tom ordered, "give me the time lag between laser blasts. How long do they take to recharge?" Even as he spoke, Tom counterattacked, moving a set of cross hairs across the battle board screen with a joystick. He pressed the button on top of the stick, and the fire-control computer did the rest. The laser cannons in the Rover's nose slugged the Black Dragon's weapon.

The remaining laser fired on them again. "Thirty seconds recharge time," Rob reported. "We can't take much more of this.

Skin sensors show a patch of armor is on the verge of melting."

Tom placed an explosive charge in the robot's hand. "Think you can make it to that wall in twenty seconds?" he asked.

Rob was out of the access hatch before Tom had finished the question. He charged with incredible speed across the free-fire field. Reaching the wall, he bounded into the air, his arms raised like a basketball player making a slam dunk. The robot triggered the charge and hurled it at the base of the laser mast, even as the cannon on the top swiveled down to aim at him.

With two seconds to spare, the charge went off, tearing a hole in the wall. Behind it, the laser mast toppled like a felled tree.

"Great work, Rob," Tom said into his mike as the robot sprinted back. "Now give us a push to let the treads dig in." They felt the Rover shift, and Phil gunned the engines. For a second, the treads just spun. Then they caught, and the vehicle lurched for the hole in the wall, with Rob running behind.

The cleanup crew of human guards expected to find only wreckage in the free-fire zone. From the looks on their faces, they weren't ready to face an unharmed, battle-ready Rover. The men scattered, their squad leader bawling for assistance into his helmet mike.

Tom had to take care of these guys before that help arrived. He cracked the access hatch and tossed a sonic grenade, taking out the left half of their battle line.

One sharpshooter actually managed to get an electronic dart through the narrow opening. It hit Tom's arm, but the nonconductive Kevlar did its work. The dart bounced off, its charge hissing uselessly on the Rover's metal floor.

Another squad member appeared on a robot ramp overhead, a demolition charge in one hand. He dropped it on the minitank, but Rob intercepted the deadly package and tossed it aside, so that it exploded harmlessly.

Now the guards began to draw back. They weren't running in panic, though. Someone had ordered them to retreat. Tom frowned. That didn't sound like the Black Dragon's style. He wouldn't mind throwing away the lives of his men if he could slow or disable any intruders to his domain.

Three blocks down, a left turn, and then two more blocks would bring them to the lab building. "Let's move, Phil," Tom said, "and fast."

The Rover shot forward, its turbine engines whining. Rob leapt onto the rear of the vehicle, hitching a ride.

Inside the Rover, Tom moved to the sensor board. All the scanning devices showed the same thing. Everyone—and everything—in the Black Dragon's complex was retreating toward the same point, the old administration building.

In the distance, Tom saw swarms of worker robots cease their individual scurryings. They turned, formed ranks, and marched off together. It was as if a single mind suddenly controlled them. Tom shivered. A single mind *did* control them—Xavier Mace. The disturbing question was, what did he intend to do with them?

What about a kamikaze robot attack? Tom could easily imagine a wave of the metal workers trying to overwhelm the Rover, ready to hammer, chop, and drill it into scrap. He ordered the vehicle's on-board computer to take over all defensive weapons, and then he charged up the lasers.

Tom also explained the situation to Rob. "Better come back inside," he said.

But as they zoomed through the now-empty streets, the expected attack never materialized. What is Mace up to? Tom asked himself. What has he got up his sleeve?

Then, ahead of them, they saw the small lab building that was their target.

Rob, back on the sensors, reported, "The entire place is surrounded by a high-energy electron field."

"Well, if Mace expects that to fry me, he's in for a big disappointment," Tom said. He reached for the access door, then stopped, frowning. "It's too easy. There must be a trap. Any signs of snipers hiding on nearby roof-tops? Maybe there's another electronic mine set in the doorway."

"Nothing at all like that, Tom," Rob said. "I detect only the electron field. And there are faint traces of a human presence inside the walls."

"Rick!" Tom said. "Well, the longer we wait, the more time we give the Black Dragon to get something unpleasant ready. Cover us, Phil. Rob and I are going in."

He moved complete command of all sys-tems to Phil's control panel, then opened the access hatch. In a moment, he stood outside the lab building, his duffel bag in hand and Rob by his side.

"Nothing's happening," Tom said as they walked toward the door. He pulled another little white disk out of his bag and stuffed it down the data slot. Again, the locking mecha-nism went crazy, and the door slid half open.

A white-faced Rick Cantwell stood in the center of the room. His fists were clenched, and an ugly bruise stretched from his cheek to the line of his jaw. "I'm ready for you this time, Cougar—"

His words cut off as he recognized the robot in the doorway. "Rob?" he said, the word mingling disbelief and delight. "Where's—?"

Tom lifted the visor on his helmet.

Rick's shoulders slumped in relief. "About time you came to get me." He started to grin, but it obviously hurt his face. "How'd you get in here without getting burnt to a crisp? There's about ninety million volts of electricity outside."

"I don't have to worry about that in this suit," Tom said. "But you will." He reached into his bag of tricks. "We'll just have to—"

The huge screen on the wall flashed to life, revealing the face of the Black Dragon. "Do I have the pleasure of talking to Tom Swift?" he asked.

"You do," Tom told him. "Though I don't know why it should please you."

"It's always a pleasure to talk to someone who invents an elegant solution to a difficult problem," Xavier Mace said with a smile. "In reverse engineering the samples I obtained, I came to a lively appreciation of your genius. That's why I'm giving you this warning."

The face on the viewscreen leaned forward a little. "The secret of your superconductor is no longer a secret. My automated work force is already producing a selection of attack robots using the new technology."

Mace's smile became wider. "You have one minute to surrender, Tom Swift."

14

D**O YOU EXPECT—" TOM BEGAN, BUT THE** Black Dragon cut him off.

"Fifty-eight and a half seconds. You can believe anything you like. But if you wish to surrender, simply step outside the building and put that duffel on the ground. You have forty-five seconds left."

The viewscreen abruptly went dark.

"Tom, that guy may be crazy, but I don't think he's bluffing," Rick said. "He had little scale models of those attack robots he mentioned, using pieces scavenged from the experimental stuff he stole. I saw them. If he really has figured out how to make your superconductor—"

"We'll know in about half a minute," Tom

said, looking at his watch. "Well, I'm not going to hang around here just on his say-so."

Tom began sorting through his duffel bag, selecting the equipment he was going to use. "First," he said, "we'll kill the field around this building. Then we'll get you into our tank outside and out of this madhouse. We can—"

An explosion from outside cut off the rest of whatever he was going to say. Flipping down his visor, Tom ran to the open doorway, to find the worst of Rick's fears confronting them.

Halfway down the block, a mass of shiny spheres about the size of beach balls filled the street from wall to wall. Several lay on the ground, sliced by the Rover's laser cannon. More were in pieces, apparently blown up when the beam touched a sphere filled with explosive. But these were a mere handful compared to the number of spheres still intact. And all those balls floated in midair, about three feet off the ground.

"Tom," Phil Radnor's worried voice crackled over the helmet earphones, "what are we going to do? It looks as if Mace not only knows how to use your secret, he's put it into mass production. What—"

In a single rush, the robot spheres moved to the attack. They came forward in a wave, and now Tom discovered the secret of their mobility. The bottom portion of each globe was equipped with a rotating spray attachment. As the robot moved forward, the spray revolved, squirting a circle under itself. Thus, each robot had an electromagnetic ring under it—and a trail of interlocking rings marking the path it had taken to get there.

The street rang with the sounds of a full-fledged war. Laser cannons flashing, the Rover sent burst after burst crisscrossing down the road. It was as if two giant knives slashed through the onrushing robots. Dozens of spheres fell, slashed open. Several more exploded. One, loaded with corrosive gas, dissolved several of its neighbors and knocked several more out of the air by destroying their charged electromagnetic trails.

But there were still more than enough to mob the Rover. Some threw armor-piercing slugs. Others rammed into the vehicle and exploded. An acid-ball burnt away a laser cannon.

The vehicle tried to defend itself with the remaining cannon and butterfly bomblets, but there were just too many attackers. Huge numbers of attack spheres fell to the ground, sliced or shattered, but twice as many flew up to take their places.

When the second laser cannon was blown off by a flying bomb, Tom yelled, "Get out of here, Phil, before they kill you!"

The Rover's engines howled as Phil took off

in reverse at top speed, escaping from his hopeless position.

Tom was reminded of the danger of his own position when a ricocheting slug slammed into the door frame beside his head. He ducked for cover behind the two-inch-thick steel door, cutting off his last view of the retreating Rover. The vehicle looked as if it were being pursued by a posse of angry balloons.

No sooner had Tom jumped inside than the viewscreen flicked on again. "It seems as if your ride home had to leave the area unexpectedly," the Black Dragon said. "Perhaps you might want to reconsider some of your earlier rash words about what I can and cannot do, Mr. Swift."

Xavier Mace was still playing the game of being a considerate host. "And you may also want to reconsider my generous offer to let you surrender."

"And if I don't?"

"You face a much less agreeable option. My attack robots will wipe you out."

Already Tom could see a new force of the featureless globes gathering in the streets outside.

"Really, Mr. Swift—may I call you Tom? I think I shall. Tom, you could be a valuable addition to my organization. It's so rare for people like us to find intellects of equal stature. Your father is the only one who comes to mind. And I'm sure you'd have to agree with me, he suffers from a certain ... inflexibility ... in dealing with the world as it really is. You, on the other hand, are a younger man. There's the possibility of teaching you ..."

As the Black Dragon spoke on, Tom whispered, "Rob, smash that screen, please."

The robot swung a metal fist so hard that he not only shattered the picture tube, but crushed several of the components behind it.

"Are you sure that was a smart thing to do, Tom?" Rick asked. "The guy wanted to talk."

"That was a two-way communications link," Tom said, "and the last thing we need right now is his eyes in this room." He turned to the robot. "Rob, give me a sensor scan of this room. Any other bugging devices? Search and destroy, Rob."

That reminded Rick of his earlier conversation with the Black Dragon. "You can never be sure of what this guy knows. He told me that you'd unmasked one of his spies at Swift Enterprises," Rick said. "*One* of his spies, that's the way he put it. Suppose he has more?"

"We'll worry about that when we get home." Tom watched as Rob strolled in a circle around the room. "Well?"

"He has a bug *here* ..." Rob's fist smashed into a point about six feet up on the wall opposite the door. ". . . and *here*." Hardly bending his knees, the robot leapt twelve feet into the air to smash a spot on the ceiling. "Otherwise, the place is clean."

"Good. Now see what you can do about getting the door shut," Tom said. "I know I shorted out the machinery, but if you give it a try . . ."

While Rob dragged the broken door along its track, Tom knelt on the lab's concrete floor, sorting the contents of his duffel bag into three piles.

"What are you doing?" Rick asked, looking over his friend's shoulder.

"This stuff," Tom said, pointing to the largest pile, "will be useless in this situation. It's for knocking out human opponents or sending smoke into their eyes or distracting them with loud noises."

Then he indicated a smaller pile. "This stuff works against robots. I've got five explosive charges left, and a hand-held version of a gizmo I put in the Rover. It jams radio controls, which should result in a bunch of robots floating around aimlessly and crashing into one another."

"That's not a whole lot if we're fighting a siege," Rick said. "Especially since we don't know how long—or *if*—help will be on the way." He looked at the third pile. "What's this stuff?" he asked. "Some of it looks like that broadcast power rig you were fooling around with. I recognize the ruby rod attachment for the laser, and this looks like a tuning modulator . . ."

"Got it in one," Tom said. "I just hope it will get us out of this mess. You see, when the Black Dragon kidnapped you, I had to reexamine my whole superconductor concept. I'd made it work, so how could I make it *not* work? I could have used you around the lab, Rick—it was a real 'test to destruction' situation."

Tom grinned a little sourly, then continued. "Anyway, I learned something very unpleasant about my solid electricity crystals. Within certain limits, they work just fine. But if they get a power surge or if they're excited with a powerful blast of certain radiation frequencies, they become unstable."

"How unstable?"

"*Very* unstable. They blow up. And the energy release goes from crystal to crystal, in a sort of chain reaction."

"Awesome," Rick said, staring out the window at the ever-thickening ranks of attack robots—and at the ever-thickening superconductor trails they were laying down. Trails, he realized, that were laced with potentially unstable solid electricity crystals.

"Of course, there's a problem," Tom said. "To start this chain reaction, I need a big burst of energy, bigger than any portable power supply could provide. So I brought my broadcast power rig, figuring I could tap into a line somewhere in the complex."

He sighed. "I didn't anticipate being trapped in a room with no outlets and no major power source, except a viewscreen connection that could hardly juice a nightlight."

"What are you going to do?" Rick asked.

"Come up with something, I hope," Tom said. "I'll try to gain time by negotiating with the Black Dragon. If that doesn't work, well, we may lose, but we'll go down fighting." He looked over their pitifully small collection of weapons. "Which do you want to defend, one of the windows or the door?"

"I'll take a window, please, after you or Rob break it open. That may be safe for you guys to do, but not for me. That window's electron field—"

"Is filled with ninety million volts—and it will come right through the glass and frame!" Tom said, staring at his friend. "Rick, you are a genius!"

Remembering what his mother had said about Xavier Mace, Tom wasn't surprised when the Black Dragon made one final effort to negotiate.

A new figure floated out of the ranks surrounding the embattled lab building. This robot was specially designed for communications work. A viewscreen took up most of its round body, and loudspeakers flanked its vision gear.

Xavier Mace's heavily amplified voice boomed over the whole complex. "That was very rude, Swift, not to mention dangerous. I hold you in the palm of my hand right now—and unless you give me a good reason not to, I'm about to crush you."

Tom hurriedly assembled the components of his broadcast energy rig, hitching in a thick piece of copper cable with the insulation scraped off the end.

"Ready—let's hope we have their range," he said. Going to a window, he smashed the glass. "Mace!" Tom yelled. "If I surrender, do I have your word that you won't harm either of us?" As he spoke, he cleared the glass away from the window frame. His nonconducting spray still protected him. The frame crackled as networks of reddish sparks ran across the metal where he touched it, but Tom felt only a slight tickling sensation.

"You have my word on it," the Black Dragon promised.

Tom held the ruby rod and components in one hand and the live edge of the cable in the other. "I don't trust you," he called.

"Then you can kiss your life goodbye," said Xavier Mace.

"And you can kiss my superconductor goodbye!" Tom jammed the end of the cable against the metal window frame and was nearly hurled back by the jolt of energy that poured up the copper. The heavy wire itself began to glow, and even through his insulated suit Tom's hands felt blazing hot.

He gritted his teeth against the scorching heat, held out the ruby rod, and flicked the on switch. A beam of blindingly intense light speared out of the rod he held in his hand. Concentrated energy was being broadcast. The beam hit the ground near Mace's speaking robot. Keeping his eyes squeezed nearly shut against the glare, Tom directed the power beam onto the machine's superconductor trail.

It was like throwing a match on a trail of gasoline. The ground under the robot erupted in an eye-searing explosion, an explosion that ripped backward along the path the machine had left.

Tom turned his face from the window, afraid the infrared radiation coming in through his helmet visor might burn his eyes out. Blindly, he played the power beam under the massed ranks of the attack robots. Explosions tore the street apart. Shock waves smashed into the robots above, twisting and crumpling them, and blasting them to pieces.

In an instant, the metal army had been turned into useless scrap. But the explosions continued, ripping their way after the detachment that had pursued the Rover, then backtracking toward the manufacturing facility where the robots had been made. Finally it reached the power plant—and two full acres of the Black Dragon's complex disappeared that night.

Tom boosted the broadcast power on his helmet radio and called Phil Radnor. "Tom!" a faint voice came to his earphones. "Those killer balls—all of them have blown up! What happened?"

"Let's say Xavier Mace has gone out of the superconductor business," Tom replied. "Come on back. He's run out of robots—"

A blasting charge blew in the lab door. Rick hit the ground, stunned. Rob was smashed down, and Tom hit the wall hard.

A black-clad figure with long pale hair leapt into the room.

"Never send a robot," Cougar said, "to do a man's job."

15

TOM LAY SLUMPED GROGGILY AGAINST THE wall, able only to stare as Cougar stepped slowly toward him, grinning expectantly.

"They told me about that supersuit you're wearing, how it's stopped most of the stuff we've thrown at you. But I think this high-tech pigsticker will be able to handle it."

A high-pitched whine assaulted Tom's ears, the kind of sound that he usually associated with a dentist's drill. Now it was coming from Cougar's right hand. The hired killer held up a knife with a larger-than-usual handle—and a blade that seemed to blur.

"The big brains call this a vibroblade," Cougar told him. "It moves so fast, it gives off ultrasonic vibrations. Gives me a headache just to hold it—but it will hurt you a lot more." The man's pale eyes actually seemed to glow with anticipation. "I've seen this sucker used to slice up diamonds. So I can hardly wait to experiment a little on that fancy suit of yours."

Tom had no illusions about how his suit would stand up to Cougar's "experiment." Desperately, he struggled, trying at least to get on his feet to defend himself. But he could hardly move.

Cougar gave a cold laugh. "This is going to be almost too easy," he said. "One for the record books—Cougar succeeds where the Black Dragon fails."

Tom glanced at the floor, where the arsenal from his duffel bag was now scattered. If only one of his sonic grenades were around, then he could give this guy a *real* headache.

But that stuff was all in the middle of the floor. Nothing was there by the wall. Wait— something had rolled by his right foot. Pretending to hang his head in defeat, Tom took a closer look—and saw a smoke bomb!

Cougar was almost on top of him. It was now or never. Tom stomped down hard with his foot.

Billows of silver white smoke suddenly filled the room. Cougar cursed, hacking blindly toward the wall with the vibroblade. But Tom wasn't there anymore. He'd thrown himself to the right and rolled into a crouch. Thanks to his infrared visor, he could see perfectly through the smoke. That also meant he could see how the vibroblade had just sliced through solid concrete as if it were soft cheese.

Cougar's teeth were bared in a silent snarl. He strained, listening for the faintest sound to guide his blade in another slash. Staying low, Tom circled silently to his right, trying to find an opening where he could leap in and try to disarm the guy.

Fast as a striking cat, Cougar slashed toward the noise. Tom frantically backpedaled, the blade passing within inches of his chest. The knife was still between him and Cougar.

The man in black was good with edged weapons—very good. Even fighting blind, he might back Tom into a wall or corner, or get lucky with one of those stabs. Tom had to jump him, and now.

Rick beat him to the punch. He, too, had been knocked to the floor by the blast at the door. He'd stayed there, and as the smoke cleared from the bottom up, he'd recognized Cougar's cowboy boots—and with all the skill and strength he'd gained on the football field, Rick tackled.

But Cougar had some sort of criminal sixth sense and moved slightly as Rick dove. The result was that Rick got only one foot in his tackle. He quickly got Cougar's other one in his face.

"Hey, that's your pal, Swift." Abruptly, Cougar switched off the vibroblade and scooped up Rick. Before Tom could get to them, the thug and his captive had smashed through the remaining undamaged window in the lab.

Tom took a split second to grab up some of his arsenal. "Rob," he commanded. "Up and after me!"

A corner of the steel door rose from the floor, and Rob slid out from under. "Still more dents," he lamented.

Tom and his robot leapt from the doorway into the darkness outside. The only lights in the area were in the old administration building.

Right, Tom remembered. The admin building had a separate power source for emergencies. Now it looked as if the Black Dragon was using it—and Mace's top thug was heading there.

Cougar had adopted the classic terrorist/ hostage position with Rick. He backed along with his captive standing in front of him, the vibroblade at Rick's throat.

They went into the building through the door to what Tom remembered as the old analysis laboratory. He peered into a window to see that his memory was correct—Cougar and Rick were retreating down one of the many aisles between the lab tables.

"Rob," Tom whispered to his robot, "after we go through the door, we split up. The idea is to come at this guy from two different directions."

They burst through the entrance. Rob went right, Tom went left. Tom ran full speed down an aisle that paralleled Cougar's course.

"Hold it, Swift," the thug yelled. "You forget who's got the upper hand."

Tom skidded to a halt as Cougar menaced Rick with the vibroblade. "Rob! Stop!" he called.

"Now, Swift, if you or your tin friend make another move, your buddy here will have a lot more to worry about than some bumps and bruises."

Tom covertly eyed the two weapons he'd managed to snatch from the lab floor. Great. The radio jammer and demolition bomb. Why couldn't he have found a sonic grenade? They must have all been under the fallen door.

"Just to keep you from getting fidgety, Swift, I'll give you a little something to occupy your time," Cougar said. "Take off that helmet."

Tom shrugged. With the lights on in here, there was no need for the infrared visor. He undid the helmet and pulled it off. Then he saw where Cougar was heading—and why he wanted Tom bareheaded.

Two tables away from where Cougar and Rick stood was a lab table with a machine pistol on it.

Cougar followed Tom's eyes. "Yeah, it's loaded. They were testing new depleted-uranium bullets for the attack robots. You're a dangerous guy to get close to, Swift. But even though I may not be the best shot in the world, I think I can take you out from here."

Once Cougar got to that gun, Tom knew he'd be finished. Rick knew it, too. His eyes pleaded with Tom to give him a chance, some kind—*any* kind—of distraction. There was the demolition pack. An explosion would be sure to distract Cougar. Of course it might also bring down the building. And Cougar was too close to Rick with that knife. Rick could get hurt—and badly. There had to be some other way.

Tom looked at the table in front of him and saw a way. Sitting among a lot of electrical gear was the control panel that Rick had used to control his skyboard. And on a laboratory table behind Cougar, floating about a foot in the air, was the skyboard itself. Right now, the board was a collector's item. It probably

represented the only undestroyed superconductor still in the Black Dragon's hands.

Cougar and Rick had reached the lab table
with the gun. Tom's hand slipped onto the
control knob. "Cougar," he said, not finding
it too difficult to sound nervous. "Can't we
work something out?"

That actually got a smile from Cougar.
"The boss says you're history. Maybe it's
because he doesn't like competition in the
genius business. Then again, it may be
because you blew up so much of the complex
here."

His left hand reached for the gun, his right
held the knife to Rick's throat, and his eyes
darted from Tom to Rob to Rick. This was it.

Tom twisted the speed rheostat to the maximum, sending the skyboard leaping off its
magnetic field. The board flew across the
space between tables and hit Cougar hard in
the left side.

He half swung around at the unexpected
assault, his free hand fumbling for the pistol.
Rick twisted free of the knife, and Tom
launched himself for Cougar.

Smashing into the thug, Tom sent him
sprawling across the top of yet another table.
Then, grabbing Cougar's right arm, he
smashed the guy's wrist against the table
edge, once, twice, three times. The vibroblade
flew from Cougar's hand, gouging its way

down the side of the table until it crashed to the floor.

Then Rick joined the party. After all his friend had been through, Tom thought it only fair that Rick be the one finally to knock Cougar cold.

Turning off the vibroblade, Tom slipped the knife into his pocket. "Rob," he ordered, "find us something we can use to tie up this ..." Tom's voice trailed off as he stared at the gleaming robot before him. Two things were wrong.

For one thing, the last thing Tom had done before the raid was to spray Rob with the nonconducting solution. That had made the robot's metal skin dull. Equally important, where were all the dents Rob had gotten in the course of this adventure?

"All right, Mace," Tom said grimly. "What have you done to Rob?"

The robot before him sighed. "That's the problem with rush jobs. To save time, you use stock footage instead of actually copying the original." The robot was speaking in the voice of Xavier Mace.

"Still, you have to admit, this was a rather good illusion, wasn't it? As long as I stayed out of your direct vision." The image of the seven-foot-tall robot began to shimmer and dissolve.

It wavered completely for a moment, then disappeared. Behind it stood a five-foot, ten-inch grandfatherly figure both Tom and Rick had seen before.

Unmasked before them stood the Black Dragon.

MACE GAVE TOM A SOUR LOOK. "VERY POOR research, Mr. Swift. You'd have saved us all a lot of grief if you'd discovered the high-energy instability of your power crystals earlier."

"So, it's 'Mr. Swift' again," Tom said.

The Black Dragon bowed. "It's the least I can do for a worthy opponent."

"I think you can do a lot better than that," Rick said hotly. "You tried to steal Tom's invention, kidnapped me, and nearly got us killed. Then you have the nerve to act as if this were all Tom's fault for being a bad scientist!"

He began to advance on Mace, clenching and unclenching his fists. "I'll bet you're not so tough when you don't have a massive electric shock to back you up," he said. "What's to stop us from grabbing you, tying you up with Cougar, and giving the two of you to the state police as a joint package?"

"Don't hurt yourself when you tackle him," Tom advised. "He's only a hologram."

"Not this time," Rick told his friend. "I can see—" His jaw went loose, and his whole spirit deflated as he approached the smiling Mace a little closer. "I can see just the faintest outline of laboratory desk right through him."

Rick turned to Tom. "How did you guess?"

"I started to suspect when he changed images from Rob to Mace," Tom said. "For a split second, there was a flicker, and *nothing* was there. Then there's the fact that the Mace image was a little too confident that we'd never bring it to justice."

He frowned. "But that doesn't tell us what happened to Rob and where he is."

"Try your father's old office," the hologram of Xavier Mace told them. "The robot is there—and you'll see me in the flesh."

Rick looked at Tom. "What are we waiting for?"

They took a few minutes to tie up the now reviving Cougar with some electrical wire they found, then headed for the main office.

"It's weird," Tom admitted as they walked down a dimly lit corridor to the head office.

"Dad worked here for years. Now I'm going to confront Dad's worst enemy."

They stepped past the old receptionist's desk. Rick reached out to turn the handle, and the door to the office swung silently open. Tom had to stifle a gasp. The furniture, the rug, even the curtains on the walls were exactly the way they'd been when he and Mr. Swift had worked there. Somehow, the Black Dragon had even filled the display cases with models identical to the ones that had once sat on the shelves.

The only part of the picture out of place was the portly, grandfatherly figure sitting in Tom Swift, Sr.'s high-backed executive chair.

"I don't see Rob around here, Mace." Rick snatched up a silver tray from a table by the door and tossed it at the figure. "And if you're another hologram—"

The tray didn't go through the figure. It struck it in the chest, knocking it out of the chair.

Both boys ran toward the still form on the floor. "I didn't mean to—" Rick burst out. His face was pale as Tom knelt beside the figure and felt at the throat for a pulse. "Is—is he dead?"

"You might say that," Tom replied. "He was never alive."

"*What*?" Rick bent over the body and touched it. "It's a wax dummy!"

"A wax statue," Tom corrected him grimly. "An imaginary person created to look as life-like as possible. We may as well forget about passing out detailed descriptions of Xavier Mace. This is probably what he *doesn't* look like."

Seeing Rick's confusion, he explained. "The real Mace had this statue made and had holograms taken of it. Then, using computer animation, he was able to use this completely false image of himself with all of his people."

"No way," Rick objected. "You forget I was with Mace in that lab for the scale-model experiment with the attack robots. He was a real guy. Those were real marbles he pulled out of his pocket, and those were real toy soldiers they knocked over. I *saw* that. Cougar threw me on the floor. I landed on some of them."

"Very good point, Rick," Xavier Mace's voice said. They whirled to find another hologram image of the Black Dragon shimmering into existence by the office door.

"I'm sorry to say you were the victim of an elaborate hoax," Mace went on. "Yes, a real person scattered those model robots over the track. It was one of my security guards. A hologram was projected over his body to make him look like me." The false Mace smiled. "I'm afraid the real me left this complex—and New York State—some time ago."

The incredibly lifelike figure stepped in front of the door. "This complex will be too much in the public eye in the near future," it explained. "Too many mysterious events—explosions in the night and so forth. Of course, it's all right. This is a completely automated operation. But some of the locals will complain that it's not safe for the town. So I'll leave."

"To come back sometime later with another face and another name to run things," Tom said.

"Exactly." The image shifted, growing bigger and taller—turning into Rob, in fact. "You see how easy it is."

"I'm confused. How does he keep growing and shrinking like that?" Rick asked.

"It's the hologram image that grows and shrinks," Tom said, "or makes things invisible. If I stood by the wall and had a hologram of just the wall played over me, you wouldn't see me."

"But is that a hologram of Rob?" Rick asked, "or is it the real thing?" He walked toward the robot.

"Oh, it's the real Rob all right," the robot assured him, still using Mace's voice. A huge hand reached out as Rick made for the door, shoving him back.

Rick went pale. "That is the real Rob," he

said. "So why is he talking with Mace's voice?"

"I'm preparing one final mystery for tonight's events," the robot said. "The two young intruders—Rick Cantwell and Tom Swift—who'll be found dead in Tom's father's old office after their robot went berserk."

"Tom, what are we going to do?" Rick said.

"Say your prayers," Rob suggested. "You know how well protected this office is, and I'm standing between you and the only door."

"So you're the other spy in Swift Enterprises," Tom said calmly, putting his hands in his pockets. "I suppose Garret Frayne programmed you, too."

"Oh, no," Rob said in Mace's voice. "*Orb* programmed me. Frayne did indeed reprogram Orb, but his most important job was inserting a piece of hardware into Orb's circuitry. It's a simple little microchip that looks like thousands of others inside Orb. This particular chip, however, gives Xavier Mace a back door into all of Orb's operating systems. Now that the chip is in, Orb can be reprogrammed even from a distance, to do almost anything."

Mace's voice laughed at them. "And the best thing is, it's virtually undetectable! The Swift Enterprises computer people purged all of Orb's software and reprogrammed him.

But they left the vital piece of hardware unchanged."

The robot was nearly on top of them now. "Well," Mace's voice said, "I've satisfied your curiosity. Now let's get this done with."

"Right." Tom stepped right into the robot's path. In one quick movement, he whipped out the vibroblade. The dentist-drill whine turned into a higher-pitched shriek as the blade sliced through the metal arm reaching for him. Rob's other arm moved to crush Tom to the robot's chest, but Tom ducked, slashing the vibroblade through Rob's midsection.

For a second, the robot stopped in its tracks, its photocell "eyes" seeming to blink in confusion. Then Rob fell to the floor with a crash.

"Rob's brain is actually in his stomach," Tom explained to Rick, who stood frozen, goggling at the spectacle. "The head is just full of sensor gear." He stepped over the metallic figure and strode to the door. "Let's get my helmet back and call Phil Radnor. We're not out of this yet."

Rick stepped out of the office. As Tom went to close the door, he looked back sadly. "Sorry, Rob," he whispered.

"Are you sure this is all going to work out?" Rick asked as they flew the Rover back to California.

"No," Tom said seriously. "We can't call anyone back home to warn them about Orb, because Orb is tied into all our communications networks. We're close enough to home now for me to try sneaking into the system to find out exactly where in the complex Orb is. The problem is, I need all our on-board computer capacity to get past our safeguards. That means you'll have to fly the plane in the beginning of the descent. I'll take over for the actual landing."

Tom smiled at the look on his friend's face. "Come on, yours is the easiest job! Think of Phil Radnor, having to convince Cougar to help him get Rob off the Black Dragon's property before the authorities finally arrive."

"We promised to let Cougar go," Rick said.

"And if he's smart, he'll disappear. It's not smart to get the Black Dragon mad at you."

Rick shuddered. "*That* I already know."

"Phil will try to keep the Lake Carlopa thing hushed up," Tom went on. "Mace may be a little surprised when the media don't play up the whole gory story, but it may give us just enough time to land and then neutralize Orb."

"Right," Rick said. "We don't want Mace to realize we're alive and then use Orb for one last shot at revenge."

They managed to put off actually identifying themselves until they were in the landing pattern at the Swift Enterprises airport, joining the rest of the midmorning air traffic. Tom's father got on the radio. "Why didn't you tell us you were heading home with Rick? Your mother and I have been half crazy with worry!"

"Sorry, Dad," Tom replied. "I thought it was best to keep it a secret until we'd actually landed."

"Well, you can prepare yourself for a welcome. Your sister is home from the hospital, and we'll all be waiting for you at the robotic hangar."

That was the top of the line for plane maintenance at Swift Enterprises. The entire hangar was run by computer, with automated cranes and robot welding arms performing plane maintenance and repair.

"That's great," Tom said as he signed off. But where is Orb? he thought. In spite of his best efforts over the last hour, he hadn't been able to track the robot. His search program was still running, though, and Tom had hopes he'd know where Orb was by the time he and Rick landed.

The landing was not a smooth one. Tom was just too tired. The Rover bounced three times on the runway.

"Looks like we'll have to overhaul the onboard computer," Tom's father complained.

"It should have landed the plane better than that."

Tom taxied toward the hangar, whose doors opened automatically. Inside were Tom's parents, as well as the Cantwells. Mandy stood waving up at the cockpit, her arm around Sandra, who looked pale but happy, at least the little of her he could see with one of the robot welding arms in his way.

"Orb located," the on-board computer announced.

"Finally," Tom said.

But as the plane taxied all the way into the hangar, he didn't need the information anymore. Tom could see exactly where Orb was—in his sister's arms, right in the middle of the computer-controlled hangar.

Then Tom realized that the hangar doors were closing and that something was moving out from the repair equipment folded against the wall.

A huge robot welding arm was moving toward his family!

Tom DIDN'T EVEN STOP TO THINK. WITH THE
plane still moving, he yelled, "Take over the
controls, Rick!"

His left hand shoved open the canopy, and
his right darted into his breast pocket for the
needle he'd magnetically encoded back at
Phil Radnor's place. He stood on the wing,
ready to jump down to Sandra and deactivate
Orb. All his attention was on the little round
robot.

In fact, he was so intent on Orb, he didn't
even notice the crane arm that suddenly
swung into motion to brush him off the wing.

A yell from Mandy of "Tom! Behind you!"
was the only warning he got.

It wasn't enough. He didn't fall, but

although he managed to grab on to the crane, the magnetized needle was knocked from his hand. It fell to the hangar floor, its noise unnoticeable in the thunder of the reversing engines.

But everyone noticed that the crane arm was now swinging up, taking Tom with it.

"Tom! What's—"

"Something's wrong!"

"—the controls!"

"Tom!"

Over the confused babble, he could hear his mother's anguished cry as he let go of the crane.

He'd calculated things correctly, though. He dropped onto the raised tail of the Rover just as it passed by.

Tom scrambled along the body of the plane, waving frantically to Sandra.

"Sandra! Take Orb—"

A warning Klaxon began a deafening hooting, drowning out his words.

Tom could see Sandra's lips moving. "I can't hear you," she was saying.

At least the welding arm was moving away from her. Now it was heading for the magnetized needle on the floor.

"Sandra!" he yelled desperately.

His sister stared up at him, her face pale and confused.

Tom had reached the pilot's ladder behind

the wing. The deactivation needle was only about five feet below him.

The welding arm got to it first.

Its electric arc spat a giant spark, filling the hangar with the stink of ozone. The needle melted into a shapeless mass.

But Tom was paying no attention to the needle. He threw himself across the wing, shouting in the sudden silence, "Sandra! Throw Orb to me!"

Sandra trusted her brother. She tossed him the round robot, throwing it underhand as if it were a giant softball.

Tom realized that either she had underestimated Orb's weight or overestimated her strength. The robot would end up just a little short of Tom's outstretched hands.

Tom belly flopped on the wing and managed to snatch Orb out of the air. He also noticed that the welding arm, the crane, and a huge ceiling-mounted winch were all converging on the Swifts and Cantwells. Tom sat up on the wing, Orb in his lap. With sweaty hands, he examined Orb's silvery skin for the telltale pinhole.

The light was suddenly blocked out from above him as the crane once again came swinging down, this time aiming for his head. Tom's hand darted for his breast pocket once more, pulling out another deactivation pin.

He forced himself not to look and see how

close the welding arm had come to Mandy and Sandra. Nor did he spare a second to glance at the killing blow coming down on him.

All of Tom's attention went to shoving that magnetized needle home.

It slid in.

All the machinery stopped in its tracks.

Tom Swift let out a long, shuddering sigh.

Outside in the bright sunshine, the welcoming party stood in shocked silence as Tom and Rick told what they had learned at Lake Carlopa—and explained the awful tragedy they'd just averted in the hangar.

"You're a real hero," Sandra added.

"Xavier Mace is a brilliant, vengeful man," Tom's mother finally said. "It's a good thing you thought to bring an extra deactivating needle."

"I magnetized *three* needles and brought them along," Tom explained, "just in case."

He patted the breast pocket of his flight suit, then went deathly pale when he realized it was empty.

"That belly flop on the wing," he said in a thin voice. "The third needle must have fallen out then."

"It doesn't matter," Mandy said, putting her arms around him. "You managed to outwit Orb, and you still had a needle to turn him off. That makes you a hero."

"A *lucky* hero," Tom pointed out.

"My favorite kind," Mandy told him. "And I think you deserve a hero's welcome." She threw her arms around Tom, gave him a major hug, then kissed him. "After all, it's the least I can do for the guy who saved my life."

Mr. Swift, in the meanwhile, was already getting on the phone to Phil Radnor, promising him any help he might need in handling the Lake Carlopa incident.

"You should have your people on the lookout for Garret Frayne," he told the government man. "Harlan Ames, my head of security, reports that he's disappeared." Mr. Swift hit a button to turn on the speaker.

"If he has any brains, he's not only on the run from the police, but probably hiding out from the Black Dragon, too," Phil Radnor's voice said. "Mace is quite ruthless with people who might testify against him."

"But what about the Black Dragon?" Rick asked. "Aren't you going to get him arrested, Mr. Radnor?"

"For what?" Phil Radnor's voice reflected the weariness of five years of combat. "Mace himself didn't kidnap you. And there's sure to be no proof of any connection between him and Cougar."

Mr. Swift thanked his friend, then hung up.

"We know Mace isn't at Lake Carlopa now," Tom said.

"And you can bet that if the police were to start asking questions, Mace would have an alibi all ready. Probably a platoon of respectable, powerful citizens will step up to swear he was nowhere near Lake Carlopa for the whole past month. I'm sorry," Mr. Swift said. "But that's the way it is. There are enough greedy people in the world to help men like Mace get away with anything he'll pay for."

"Well," Mandy said, "I guess we should be glad there are a few people like you and Tom around, to give the bad guys a hard time."

Tom grinned. "We did, didn't we? And there's one other good thing to come out of this."

"What's that?" Rick asked.

"We learned that my new superconductor is too unsafe to use."

"That's the *good* news?" Mr. Swift said.

"Well, we half destroyed the Black Dragon's headquarters finding it out," Tom finished.

That got a laugh from everybody.

"And, of course," Mr. Swift said, smiling, "you don't have to work on those cost projections."

"Back to the drawing board," Tom agreed, stretching in an enormous yawn. "But I think I'll take it easy today." He turned to Mandy.

"What do you think of going to the beach? I bet you can borrow one of Sandra's bathing suits."

"Sounds good to me," she said, putting her arm through his.

As they loaded up Tom's car, Mandy sighed, looking at the skyboard in the backseat. "You know, I'm going to miss the idea of the two of us riding off into the sunset on that thing."

"To tell the truth, I'll miss it, too." Tom shrugged. "But there's one thing you learn early in my family."

"What's that?" Mandy asked.

Tom Swift smiled at her. "There's always a *next* invention."

Tom's next adventure:

Teen inventor Tom Swift is determined to re-create in miniature one of the most powerful forces in nature: a black hole. But Tom loses control of the experiment. He's sucked through the hole into a parallel universe, exchanging places with his perfect double—a criminal mastermind targeted for revenge by a powerful government agent.

On the lam from the law, Tom must find a way back home. Otherwise he'll remain a hunted man for the rest of his life, and his own world will fall prey to his alter ego—a twisted genius at the helm of Swift Enterprises, steering a course toward unlimited wealth, unlimited power, and unlimited evil . . . in Tom Swift #2, *The Negative Zone*.

ENTER THE TOM SWIFT SWEEPSTAKES!
1 GRAND PRIZE: Macintosh® Classic®
Personal Computer
10 FIRST PRIZES: BMX RANDOR BICYCLE

Entry limited to 17 years of age and under.
All entries must be received by 5/1/91.

Official Sweepstakes Rules

NO PURCHASE NECESSARY. To enter, fill out entry form available at participating retailers during the promotional period; or fill out entry form in the back of <u>The Black Dragon</u> and <u>The Negative Zone</u>, Archway Paperbacks' books published by Pocket Books, available at participating retailers during the promotional period; or hand print your name, address, zip code, age and phone number on a post card and mail it to:

TOM SWIFT SWEEPSTAKES, Archway Paperbacks, Dept. TSS
1230 Avenue of the Americas, New York, NY 10020

Enter as often as you wish. Each entry form must be mailed separately. Entrants must be 17 years of age and under. All entries must be received by May 1, 1991 Photocopies or other mechanical reproductions of completed entries will not be accepted Simon & Schuster, Inc. is not responsible for lost, misdirected or late mail.

All winners will be selected at random. All interpretations of the rules and decisions by Simon & Schuster, Inc. are final. All winners will be selected from among entries received by May 1, 1991. Drawing will be held on or about May 15, 1991 Winners will be notified by telephone or mail. Odds of winning will be determined by the total number of entries received.

The estimated value of the Grand Prize, an Apple Macintosh® Classic® personal computer, including monitor, keyboard, mouse, and system software, is $999.00. There are ten first prizes and the estimated retail price per first prize of a BMX Randor Boys bike is $90.00. Arrangements for the grand prize and first prize fulfillment to be made by Simon & Schuster, Inc.

Prizes are nontransferable. Taxes on all prizes awarded will be the sole responsibility of the winners. Simon & Schuster, Inc. reserves the right to substitute prizes of a value approximately comparable to that exhibited in the promotional campaign, or the cash equivalent to Simon & Schuster, Inc's estimated retail value of obtaining the prize, if for any reason Simon & Schuster, Inc. is unable to furnish the specific items described.

Sweepstakes open to citizens and residents of the United States and Canada, 17 years of age and under, except employees and their families of Apple Computer, Inc., Simon & Schuster, Inc., affiliated companies, subsidiaries, advertising and promotional agencies and participating retailers. Void where prohibited by law.

In order to win a prize, residents of Canada will be required to correctly answer a skill question administered by mail Any litigation respecting the conduct and awarding of a prize in this publicity contest by a resident of the province of Quebec may be submitted to the regie des loteries et courses du Quebec.

Each prize winner and/or his/her parent or legal guardian will be required to sign and return an Affidavit of Eligibility and compliance with official rules, within thirty (30) days of notification attempt. Noncompliance within this time period will result in disqualification and an alternate winner will be selected. Grand prize winner may be requested to consent to use of name and likeness for publicity and advertising.

For a list of Sweepstakes winners (available August 15, 1991), send a self-addressed, stamped envelope to:

TOM SWIFT WINNERS, Archway Paperbacks, Dept. TSW
1230 Avenue of the Americas, New York, NY 10020

Tom Swift is a registered trademark of Simon & Schuster, Inc.
© 1990 Apple Computer, Inc. Apple, the Apple logo, Macintosh are registered trademarks of Apple Computer, Inc.
Classic is a registered trademark licensed to Apple Computer Inc.

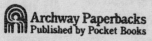
Archway Paperbacks
Published by Pocket Books

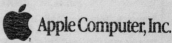
Apple Computer, Inc.

OFFICIAL ENTRY FORM

Name_____

Address_____

City_____ State_____ Zip Code_____

Phone_____ Age_____